HIDDEN TREASURE

A NOVEL

DR. STEVEN A. JIRGAL

Published by The Core Media Group, Inc., P.O. Box 2037, Indian Trail, NC 28079.

Cover design by Rock Graphics, Concord, NC.

Printed in the United States of America.

To the mentally challenged men and women of the world: We see you, we hear you, and we love you. You are not alone as you walk the path that God has laid out before you. Thank you for the joy and fullness you have brought to so many lives.

And to the caretakers: Your loving and caring hearts have not gone unnoticed. The mercy of God is yours (Matt. 5:7).

And to the teachers and members of the Christian Crusaders Community Group at Lee Park Church: May the Lord bless you richly as you continue to grow in your walk with him. There will always be room for you!

TABLE OF CONTENTS

-1-
THE NEWS

Bill and Jenny held hands as they sat in front of Dr. Kent's desk absorbing the expression on his face as he entered. Dr. Kent was a middle-aged man who had been practicing in the same office for over 20 years. He carried a serious but caring disposition and had gained a solid reputation in the community. Today his countenance was grave and carried a message of bad news. With his knee, he nudged his chair away from the desk while he pulled the report from the large green folder. A heavy sigh eased from his lungs as he settled into his chair. He had read the report earlier and spent his energies trying to figure out how to share the findings in a supportive way.

He leaned forward and glanced from one person to the other. "It seems there are some problems." He paused gathering his thoughts while searching for the exact words.

"The blood work shows that your baby has some brain dysfunction. Of course, at this point, we don't know to what extent."

The couple leaned forward as if to hear better.

"The lab tests show that your little boy has Down Syndrome."

Tears came to Jenny's eyes, and she made no attempt to stop them. She rubbed her belly as if to give the child comfort.

"Are you sure?" were the only words Bill could manage to get out.

"I'm afraid so," the doctor reluctantly replied. "I've double checked the findings and I believe they are correct."

The three occupants of the room sat for a few moments in silence as the words sank deep into the couple's hearts drawing their eyes to the floor.

Then the doctor broke the silence. "It looks like you'll have to make some special plans for the boy." He paused as if he would be asked to clarify his comment.

But Bill and Jenny knew what he might be suggesting.

Bill looked up and without glancing Jenny's way said, "Dr. Kent, Jenny and I decided a long time ago, even before we were expecting, that no matter what, we would not be going in that direction."

The doctor nodded and gave a look of understanding. "Well, you have a couple of months to go, and hopefully that will give you time to prepare." He put the report back in the folder and placed it on the side of his desk. "But I need to tell you, though we don't know the extent of the damage, life with a mentally challenged child can be very difficult. Some children never speak. Some can't walk well. Some maintain the mental level of an infant. It's important that you are ready for whatever challenges you may face.

Jenny's eyes never left the floor and her tears followed in the direction of her gaze. After several moments of silence, she gently declared, "Doctor, we know we're having a boy. And this boy will be our son. And no matter how he develops, we're going to love him as much as any parents can." As she looked at her husband, she felt the reassurance she needed in his silent nod and the gentle squeeze of his hand.

The couple left Dr. Kent's office, their heads swirling with a mixture of emotions. Although they held minute suspicions that something might be wrong, they dismissed them as normal pre-parental fears.

Now their dreams and plans would have to be adjusted to whatever time and labor delivered.

Over the next couple of years, similar conversations had taken place in multiple doctors' offices. Words like, "Down Syndrome, Abnormalities, brain dysfunction, truncated cranial development, mental deficiencies, and impeded brain development" were used to describe the condition of the pre-born children. Each report was met with disbelief, fear, sorrow, determination, resolution, and even anger. In short order, both choices and plans were made as the parents came to grips with the news.

And in time the children did come. Each with their own challenges and opportunities. Some were more severe than others and a few were mis-diagnosed possessing only minor mental flaws such as stuttering or mild attention-deficit disorder.

-2-
THE YOUNG MEN

-WAYNIE-

Bill and Jenny's son was named Waynie. Mentally, he developed to the level of a four-year-old. Physically, as is often the case, he was somewhat short and stout. Waynie was filled with enthusiasm and the *gift* of verbalizing his thoughts. If it came in, it came out. Commenting on everything he saw and felt, he was quick to share his voice with those around him. He had also developed the habit of repeating many of the comments he made. "Good to go! Good to go! Looks like we're good to go!" were words that Bill and Jenny came to expect whenever the family left the house. Likewise, he had a cache of phrases the couple became used to even to the point that they expected it. "Home again, home again jiggety jig" was repeated each time they pulled into the driveway. And when someone made a comment on the weather, they could count on, "Best weather in town."

Often, he would latch onto a word from a movie or television show, and Bill and Jenny would expect to hear that phrase multiple times over the next few days. The newly found phrase was only dismissed when it was replaced by another one. An episode from *The Andy Griffith Show* birthed a long-term phrase in Waynie and he would be heard repeating, "Nip it in the bud! Nip it in the bud! Waynie's gonna nip it in the bud!" Predictably, this was replaced by Jerry Seinfeld's greeting of his neighbor and Waynie would often repeat, "Hello Newman! Hello Newman!" Although most times phrases were replaced by other phrases or words, somehow the word *Groovy* most often surfaced in Waynie's vocabulary.

It became somewhat comical when Bill and Waynie would be nestled on the couch and a familiar show would come on. Bill would slip over to Jenny and deliver the new phrase he felt certain Waynie would pounce on. And when he was right and Waynie would deliver the predicted quip, Bill would turn toward Jenny, and both would bear bright smiles and give knowing nods.

-JOHN TUCKER-

In another part of the county, Alex and Wendy Meyer were facing the challenges of bringing up John Tucker (J.T.) who was stricken with what could be called moderately functioning autism. Aside from a few gentle noises from deep within his throat, J.T. never spoke. Although several tests revealed intact and healthy vocal cords, the words from his mind never made their way to his lips. Although he never spoke a word, his facial expressions and hand gestures informed the couple of his needs, desires, and opinions.

J.T. had mentally grown to the level of a five-year-old, but in some ways seemed much older. He had an affinity for music and was drawn to any musical instrument he heard or saw. He never caught on to the proper lip engagement with wind instruments, but seemed to understand the working of various stringed instruments such as the guitar and violin. Primarily he was captivated by the piano and seemed mesmerized by the melodies that came from the large box.

At church, J.T.'s draw to the piano was quite obvious. He seemed to be mesmerized as he listened to the introductory music being played by the pianist before the service started. Several times, when the service was over and folks would be milling around, J.T. would slip away from his mom and dad and work his way to the piano bench. The first couple of times they found him sitting at the piano just staring at the keys. He wasn't touching them, just staring at them almost with an attitude of appreciation. Eventually he began to depress the keys, but he never played any kind of tune. He seemed to simply enjoy the sound of each key.

When J.T. was about seven years old, the trio made a trip to Colorado to see several family members. In Chicago, they had a lay-over of about two hours. They made their way to the connecting gate with Alex carrying their two carry-on bags, while Wendy and John Tucker walked behind hand in hand.

Partway down the wide walkway, Wendy felt J.T. pull sharply on her arm. She reacted by pulling back, but it only increased his tug. She hadn't seen it as they walked among the crowd, but J.T. had spotted a piano opposite the rocking chairs. Several people were rocking, but the bench at the piano was vacant. The piano was a good bit larger than the one they had at church. But that did not hinder J.T. from knowing what it was.

Immediately, Wendy knew J.T.'s desire. Alex was a bit ahead of them, so she called out, "Alex, I think we have to make a slight detour." Alex turned toward them and knew right away where J.T. was pulling her.

"Alright," he agreed. "We've got plenty of time."

And with that affirmation, her son led Wendy to the piano. J.T. slid onto the bench and stared at the keys. Alex put the bags down and leaned against the edge of the large piano. Wendy sat next to J.T. and patted him on the back gently. Then J.T. rested his hands on the ivories without hitting a note. Wendy looked at Alex as if to ask, "Do you think there's more?"

Then John Tucker depressed several keys with his right hand. A smile came to his face as he moved his fingers slowly along the keyboard. He wasn't playing a tune but simply connecting each sound with the key.

J.T. had hit each of the keys at least once, even the ones at each end. Then he stared again at the entire keyboard. With his right hand in front, he began to play a tune. As he continued to play Alex and Wendy noticed two things happening. J.T. began to play sharper and with more accuracy. It also dawned on them that he was playing a few beats behind the music that was being piped in over the loudspeakers.

Wendy and Alex looked at each other in shock and amazement. Tears came to Wendy's eyes as she listened to their son connect the music in the air with the keys at his fingertips. Alex just shook his head as he listened to his son in this new world.

Those passing by paused to hear the young man play. Even those who seemed to be in a hurry slowed down as they passed. All heads and ears were drawn J.T.'s way. To see this young man who was so young play so well was nothing short of amazing. But their surprise was greatly eclipsed by Alex and Wendy's who also understood his mental limitations.

Then as abruptly as he started, John Tucker stopped. Scattered bits of applause were heard but were largely ignored by the young man. Without looking around, he slid off the bench as if to say, "Okay, let's get going." Alex looked at Wendy who just shrugged her shoulders and stood up grabbing J.T.'s hand. The three of them walked toward the gate as if nothing had happened. But both Alex and Wendy knew that their son was very special, and it showed on their faces as they moved through the airport.

As they joined the crowd moving toward the gate, Alex asked, "What was that?"

"No idea," Wendy answered as she wiped another tear from her eye. "I don't have a clue."

John Tucker just walked along beside them, showing neither a sign of amazement or bewilderment.

Even though J.T. never had a lesson, Alex and Wendy noticed that his musical ability surpassed his mental level. His left hand eventually joined his right and in time he became quite accomplished on the piano often playing the Sunday morning introductory music at their church. Though he couldn't read music, whatever he heard, he could transfer through his hands and to the keys.

-ROBERT-

Although they never met, Robert Chesterton lived in the same town as J.T. Due to Down Syndrome, Robert's level of learning and function were that of a five-year-old. His parents were Rob and Olivia Chesterton, and he had a sister named Kelsey who was three years his senior. Kelsey served as a *second mom* to Robert never hesitating to defend him against some of the older and insensitive kids.

One evening when Robert was in kindergarten and Kelsey was in third grade, the Chestertons received a call from Kelsey's teacher, Mrs. Ross. At first Olivia was somewhat alarmed and assumed there was a problem.

Mrs. Ross explained that there had been an altercation at school involving Kelsey. Apparently some fifth graders thought it would be amusing to make fun of Robert. The three boys had been ridiculing him and bullying him. Robert was understandably frightened and that's when Kelsey stepped in. When the teacher arrived, she heard Kelsey threatening the boys and watched her punctuate her warning by sharply pushing one of the boys and sticking her finger in another young man's face. Then she grabbed Robert by the hand and led her frightened brother away.

Olivia was understandably concerned. Under no circumstances did she want Robert to endure bullying, and she also didn't want her daughter fighting at school. But at the same time she had come to expect Kelsey to look after her younger brother.

Olivia began to apologize to Mrs. Ross and give assurances that she would address the issue with Kelsey. But Kelsey's teacher cut her off in mid-sentence.

"Mrs. Chesterton, please understand, I didn't call to complain to you about Kelsey's behavior. I called to tell you how proud I was of your daughter sticking up for her brother. I wish more kids would look after their siblings the way Kelsey did today. You should be very proud of her.

It took a few moments for Mrs. Ross' words to sink in. "Well, Mrs. Ross, we are very proud of her. I appreciate you calling and letting me know about it."

"Well, Kelsey's a good girl and you guys have done a great job in raising her. You have plenty of reasons to be proud of her. And as for those boys, they will be called in to the office tomorrow. We'll do our best to make sure this doesn't happen again."

"Thank you! Thank you so much for calling."

Olivia hung up the phone and leaned against the counter. "That explains a lot," she thought. "Now I know why Robert came in and told me that Kelsey was his hero."

Robert was very active in both his body and mind. He excelled in Special Olympics and the walls of his bedroom were donned with a multitude of ribbons. The first time Robert raced he ran the 100-yard dash.

Rob had taken him to the high school track one evening during the week of the race to let Robert get familiar with the area and to explain to him what was going to happen. They went to the starting line and Rob blew a whistle for Robert to start running. Robert seemed to understand what to do and began running with Rob by his side encouraging him. He stayed in his lane and ran all the way to the cone that Rob had placed at the finish line. Then a short celebration ensued.

On the morning of the race, Olivia presented Robert with a brand-new T-shirt. It was navy blue-Robert's favorite color-and had his name on the back in big white letters. The front had a white winged foot, and it instantly became Robert's favorite shirt. He wanted to wear it every day and was disappointed when he couldn't wear it to church.

Saturday morning found Robert and his family at the track. At the proper time, all the runners lined up at the starting line. When the whistle blew, Robert took a few steps off the line. But when he saw a boy next to him stop to wave at his parents, he joined him and stood and waved as well. He wasn't' even waving in the direction of his own parents, he was just helping the younger boy wave to his.

Then Robert said something to the boy-Rob and Olivia never learned what it was-and the two of them trotted to the finish line. They both earned *completion* ribbons and wore them with as much pride as if they had won the state championship. The young man's name was Evan, and he and Robert became friends meeting at several races and eating lunch in the stands together with their parents.

With some coaching from his dad, Robert learned to run undistracted and did quite well. He even won the 100 and 55 several times. Rob and Olivia were as proud of him as if it was the International Olympics.

Robert's mental release was one of imitation. If he heard an unusual voice whether it came from a celebrity or a person in the grocery store, he was quick to imitate them. He was often able to mimic their voice inflection and had many celebrities in his mental files. On more than one occasion, Robert's father had to give him the understood double pat on the back signifying that Robert was beginning to cross the line as he imitated a person in a store or restaurant. Even though Robert was slow in his mental capacities, he understood where the limits were and that he was very close to that point.

More than a few heads would turn as a particular well-known star paid a visit to Robert's mind and voice. He held on to that personality until he got tired of it and returned to just being Robert. Sometimes his grip on the person was released after a simple comment. At other times the visit would be prolonged. On more than one occasion, Robert retained the celebrity's voice and mannerisms for nearly a full day. Among his repertoire, Robert carried voices from Robin Williams, Barney Fife, John Wayne, Elvis, Clint Eastwood, Bill Clinton, Porky Pigg, and Bugs Bunny. His ability to catch a voice along with a phrase never ceased to amaze his parents.

There were noted times however, when Robert used his vocal *talent* at inappropriate times. Once, when he and Rob were driving to a friend's house to borrow a chainsaw, Rob was on the phone and never noticed the police car hidden behind a row of trees. By the time he passed him by, he was going sixty miles an hour in a forty-five mile an hour zone. He immediately slowed down, but it was too late. The blue light came on and he pulled into a side street to wait for the officer and the verdict.

The policeman came to the driver's side of the car and explained that Rob had exceeded the speed limit and asked for Rob's license. When Rob gave him his license the officer left to process the information.

While he was gone Robert asked, "Dad, are you going to jail?"

"No, Robert. But I am gonna get a ticket and have to pay a fine."

"What's a fine?"

"A fine is money you gotta pay for doing something wrong. It's like punishment."

"He shouldn't punish you dad. You're a good man."

With a sigh, Robert agreed, "Thank you son."

The officer returned and handed Rob a sheet of paper and outlined the next steps including a court date or opportunity to pay online. Rob took the paper and nodded his head in understanding.

Before the officer had time to walk away, Robert leaned toward the open window and in a loud Clint Eastwood voice shouted, "Do you feel lucky punk?"

"Excuse me?" the man growled leaning on the door on looking in.

Before his dad could explain Robert added, "Well do ya?"

Rob was quick to explain Robert's condition and the officer simply patted the top of the car, nodded, smiled and walk away.

As he got older, Robert came to a slightly better understanding of appropriate responses and seemed to have a better hold on who might not appreciate his comments.

-SCOTTY-

A trip to the edge of the county would bring you to the home of Scotty Reed and his family. Scotty lived with His dad and mom Pete and Adele and his two older sisters, Linda, and Marybeth. Due to a lack of oxygen to the brain caused by the umbilical cord wrapped around his neck, Scotty suffered from brain damage. By the time the doctor had corrected the problem, the damage had already been done.

Scotty's mental affliction put him on the level of a four-year-old. Though his brain was dysfunctional, it never stopped working. His mind seemed to constantly command his body to move. His hands and feet always seemed to be in motion. On more than one occasion Pete and Adele noticed that even in the state of slumber, Scotty's feet would twitch and his wrists would rotate his hands.

This made it difficult for them to attend certain events together. Having Scotty sit in church or remain still at the movies proved to be very difficult. They attended church as much as possible but Scotty's lack of ability to sit still brought a need to sit in the very back and often move to the lobby. Early on, the option of going to the movies had been abandoned.

They learned that if they kept him very active close to the time when he would need to sit still, his need to move would somewhat decrease. So, before church or school they had him ride the stationary bike they kept in the basement. Scotty enjoyed the activity and seemed to have some understanding of its necessity.

Although they tried to avoid relying on it too much, occasionally the family would have to resort to medication to settle some of the movement of Scotty's body. He was on a normal dose for the most part but sometimes for an unknown reason his need for activity peaked and he was almost beyond control. His arms and legs would be moving at the same time, and he would bounce around the room uncontrollably. On one occasion, Pete tried to physically control him and was rewarded with a swollen eye and a split lip delivered by the young man's elbow.

During these higher-than-normal movement times, Scotty was never angry, he was just an over-active child with energy on the level of a squirrel overdosing on caffeine. Most of the time, the family simply had to be patient and let his energy drop down to its above normal level.

They did find that along with giving him some extra pre-event activity, it was helpful to send a soft ball that he could constantly squeeze when sitting still was necessary. And there were times when Adele would have to pull out an extra ball from her purse and slip it into Scotty's other hand.

They also discovered that as he aged, his hyper-activity seemed to wane. There were even a few times when they wondered if he would grow out of it completely. But Scotty never did outgrow his need of movement. At best, with the proper levels of medication, it could be said to be mildly under control.

For each of the parents of these four men, the doctors had no definitive answers. But they all advised them to prepare for an active lifestyle and to always keep their sons within eyesight.

-3-
MS. ESTHER AND THE BRADFORD STREET HOME

Each of the boys aged in their respective environments, and their families naturally grew in their love for them and adjusted their lives to the wants and needs of these special young men. In time, all four young men developed to the point where they were able to leave their parents and be joined together in a home for mentally challenged adults.

To qualify for the home, a person had to meet the state's requirements. The adult must be:

1. Eighteen years or older.

2. Able to demonstrate acceptable levels of self-care including personal hygiene.

3. Able to learn and follow directions.

4. Mobile.

5. Able to understand language and demonstrate an ability to communicate.

Because of J.T.'s inability to speak due to his autism, he was initially denied entrance to any group home. But through the persistence of his parents, entrance was granted because of his ability to communicate through body language and facial expressions. This of course would require a certain level of learning on the part of the caregiver. He was given permission to enter a group home on a four-month trial basis after which an evaluation would be made involving the caregiver.

The home they were assigned to was on Bradford Street in Middleburg Virginia. Middleburg was a small town in Maston County about forty minutes west of Washington, D.C. It held a population of approximately 3,000 a good portion of which worked in and around the D.C. area.

The boys' home was filled with the direction, discipline, and love of Ms. Esther Snyder. Esther was a sixty-year-old black woman from Mobile Alabama whose heart was bigger than her hefty frame. Never having children of her own and losing her husband to cancer a few years after they married somehow drew her to develop a love for the boys that freely poured itself out in every aspect of her life. The young men in her care may have been stunted mentally but their minds carried no doubt that Ms. Esther loved them dearly.

The discipline she handed out was more than off-set by the love that flowed in. She somehow knew what the boys needed and when they needed it and was quick to meet all their needs and most of their wants in a loving and timely manner.

The Bradford Street home was small but adequate. It was however, no more than that. The state was very short on housing for mentally challenged adults and had bought the home in an *emergency* arrangement. It was a three-bedroom, two bath ranch, with a side porch and a small fenced-in back yard. At best, and with an optimistic outlook, the condition of the house could be labeled in *livable condition*.

The house was nestled between two other homes on a fairly quiet street. The fence in the back yard was made of solid wood slats but was in ill repair. Some of the pieces were visibly rotted and others where simply nowhere to be found. The edge of the backyard also held a large dead maple tree, a threat to the house as well as the street.

The side porch had several floorboards that needed replacing. There were more than a few windows whose sills had rotted due to water penetration and the HVAC system was sometimes insufficient in cooling the house. The sidewalk had been cracked by a tree root and the edge had risen a couple of inches above the ground. This led to dangerous stumbles by several people. There were places in the floor particularly under the bathrooms where the joists had rotted due to leaks in the plumbing. One of the sinks gave a constant drip and several parts of the exterior façade had deteriorated. The gutter on the rear side of the house was missing and the facia underneath had fallen apart.

The foundation was a major problem in that it had several cracks which transferred damage to the walls above. Some repairs had been made to it but they were not of great substance.

But the biggest problem was the roof which needed a complete overhaul. The shingles were old and had decayed greatly causing several leaks. When it rained, water would drip into the attic and spill onto the ceiling causing the drywall to be discolored and in bad need of repair. This not only damaged the ceiling but destroyed the insulation. The leak was remedied by Esther placing several cooking pots in the attic at the points where they were most needed. During a hard rain, she and the boys would have to team up to empty the pots several times to avoid more damage to the ceiling.

Esther had written a couple of letters and even made a trip to the department of social services requesting help, but their needs were either ignored or given a *band aid* remedy. The answer she received was that the funds were simply not available or that their needs were under consideration. A few inspectors had come out and checked the damage, but that's as far as it ever went. Their findings were that the house indeed was in major need of repair, but that the occupants were in no danger.

The boys' parents were very happy with Ms. Esther, but equally unhappy with the living conditions of their young men. They too, had written letters to the Social Services office but without noticeable progress. Each family visited their son every two weeks or so and always brought with them some food including the choice favorites of their son. They always felt welcomed but were sensitive to their son's need for independence.

-4-
THE EVALUATION

On a Wednesday afternoon, Esther received an expected visitor from the social services department. It had been four months since J.T. came in as a resident, and a member of the compliance group had arrived for the evaluation.

Addison Finland was a short thin woman about fifty years of age. She had a pleasant personality and a way of putting at ease whoever she was with. She had worked in various positions for the department for over nine years and had a very good grasp of what she was doing.

Esther met her at the door, "You must be Ms. Finland. They told me you'd be by today."

"And you are Ms. Snyder. Please call me Addie."

"And you can call me Esther. Can I get you some coffee or something else to drink?"

"No thank you. I'm fine."

Addie glanced around the room as the two ladies sat down at the dining room table. She pulled a file and pen from her briefcase and laid the file open in front of her.

"How are you doing today?" Addie asked.

Esther smiled and said, "I'm blessed. How about you?"

"I'm good thanks."

There was a short pause then Addie said, "Well, I'm sure you're aware that this is a very unusual situation. The state normally requires a person to verbally communicate to be eligible for supervised housing."

Esther nodded.

"So how are things going here at the house?" Addie began.

"We're doin' fine. Of course, it's an adjustment period. But all in all, I think the young men and I are getting used to each other pretty well."

"And how are things with John Thomas?"

Esther smiled and said, "He likes to be called J.T. And things are actually going better than we thought. He's a fine young man, very respectful and seems to be getting along great with the other guys. He rooms with Scotty, and I think they're gettin' to be good friends."

"How about communication? His file says he suffers from autism and doesn't talk."

"No, he doesn't talk. And he doesn't understand sign language, but his face and body tell us what he wants and how he's feeling. We're all picking up on it pretty good."

"Are there any problems, like anger or frustration on his part or the rest of you?"

Esther looked up and to her side as if in thought, "No. No I don't think so. He seems to be fitting in really good with all of us."

After each answer, Addie jotted something down on the paper before her. Then she asked, "What would you say is the functional level of his mental capacity?"

There was a pause as Esther tried to process this question. "Well, I'm not sure what all that means. I'm not trained in all that stuff. I just try to provide for the boys and help them along."

"What I mean is, how old would you say he is mentally?"

"Oh, I get you now. I think that he might be on the level of a five or six-year-old. But I don't know. Sometimes in some ways he seems older, and sometimes younger. I just don't know."

"I know that's a hard thing to judge." Then holding the pen in both hands, she asked Esther, "Esther, overall, on a scale of one to ten, how would you rate the entire situation here at the house? How the boys get along with each other, how J.T. is adjusting, and how you're doing with all of this."

Esther gave an extended pause. She smiled, took a deep breath, and said, "Well, you sure do know how to ask hard questions. I'd say overall, it's about an eight. But I think in time we'll all get used to each other and we'll be fine. Ya know, your timing is perfect, the boys will be coming home from work any..."

Esther didn't get to finish her sentence when the door flew open, and the young men bounced in. Scotty was first and announced, "Ms. Esther! We're home!"

Waynie followed with "Home again, home again, Jiggety jig!"

This brought a smile to the faces of both women.

"Hey Fellas! Good to see you! Come over here. I want you to meet somebody."

The boys came over to the table and surrounded Esther. "Guys, this is Ms. Finland. She works for social services. She's here to see how we're getting along. Why don't you each shake her hand and introduce yourselves?"

Waynie was the first to step up and extend his hand, "I'm Waynie. Nice to meet you Ms. Finland."

Addie grasped his hand replying, "You can call me Addie."

Waynie nodded and stepped aside giving Robert room. "I'm Robert. But you can call me...Robert."

That comment brought a smile from both ladies and a chuckle from Addie.

Next, Scotty slid in front of her and bounced a couple of times on his toes. He shook his arms several times before extending his hand and said, "I'm Scotty Reed. My birthday was last week." It was actually three weeks ago, but Esther didn't bother to correct him. "I'm twenty-one." He was twenty, but again, the statement went unedited.

"Nice to meet you, Scotty."

John Tucker stepped up next to Scotty and Scotty stepped aside but not back. He stood next to J.T. sharing his method of introduction, "This is J.T."

From behind J.T. Waynie spoke up, "He doesn't talk, but we know what he wants. He can tell us. He can tell us in lots of ways."

J.T. nodded, smiled, and gave Addie his hand. "It's nice to meet you John...I mean J.T."

J.T. gave two more strong nods.

"He's glad to meet you too," Waynie volunteered.

Addie turned to Esther and asked, "Is it okay if the three of us go in another room?"

Esther nodded, "Of course." Then she turned to the other three and said, "Boys, Ms. Addy needs to talk to J.T. and me alone so we're going into his and Scotty's room." Pointing to the counter she said, "You guys can grab a piece of fruit and watch some T.V. We won't be too long."

The boys each nodded and moved toward a bowl on the counter while the other three headed down the hall.

In the bedroom, the ladies sat on the chairs while J.T. sat on the edge of the lower bunk. He looked somewhat nervous.

"This is a nice room J.T." Do you like it?" Addie began.

J.T. popped his fist in his other hand and nodded. Addie took this as a *Yes*.

"Do you like the other guys who live here?"

Again, J.T. popped his fist in his other hand and nodded.

"Are you enjoying work?"

"Are you sleeping well?"

"Are you eating well?"

"Are you a happy man?"

Each question was met with J.T.'s affirmative sign.

Then Addie asked him, "Do you have any complaints?"

J.T. shook his head while passing his open hands over each other twice.

She looked at Esther. Then standing up said, "I think that's a *No*. Well, that's all I have for now. Everything here looks fine. I'll file the approval papers and you'll get your notice in the mail."

Esther and J.T. stood up as well. She extended her hand toward the woman, "Well, it was nice to meet you, Addie."

The two women shook hands and Addie said, "You too." Then turning to J.T. and extending her hand she said, "And it was nice to meet you too J.T. I hope you have a good day."

J.T. took her hand and shook it twice while nodding two times as well.

Esther and J.T. walked Addie to the front door. As she passed through the living room she said to the boys, "It was nice to meet you fellas."

Waynie and Scotty turned and said, "Nice to meet you."

Robert was locked onto the Television and didn't respond.

Esther and J.T. watched Addie go down the steps. She closed the door and turned to J.T. and said, "Very good J.T. Time for a piece of fruit."

J.T. nodded, smiled, and moved toward the kitchen while Esther moved toward the living room. She grabbed the remote from the side table and muted the television.

"Hey, no sound!" Robert said.

"Listen guys," Esther began. As the boys sat up and turned toward her. She continued, "Mrs. Finland gave J.T. a good report and I think he's gonna be able to keep livin' with us."

Waynie gave his hands a single clap and said, "That's good! That's really good!"

The other two grinned broadly while giving J.T. a thumbs up.

-5-
CELEBRATING MR. DAVIDSON

Thursday night found the boys donning jackets and ties and seated at a table with Esther. It was the retirement dinner for Mr. Davidson who had been the director of several homes in various counties around Eastern Virginia. Over the past several months, he had gotten to know both Esther and the boys very well and the young men considered him a friend. When he made both his official and his unofficial visits to their home, he always seemed to stay beyond the time it took to gather the needed information for his report.

Mr. Davidson had an active background and the boys loved hearing his stories of serving in the military, kayaking, mountain climbing, flying planes and a host of other adventures. They sat in rapt attention as he explained each story in great detail.

Before the program started, Waynie voiced his thoughts. "Mr. Davidson don't look tired to me. I don't see why he can't keep workin'."

With a half-smile and a tilt of her head in Waynie's direction, Ms. Esther said, "He's not tired. He's retired. And he's been at it a long time and has been a good friend to you boys. Now we're gonna have a good time tonight a celebrate his retirement."

All four boys nodded in agreement.

Then Waynie asked, "Will he come visit us anymore?"

Esther's smile broadened, "Probably. It won't hurt to invite him over once in a while. You know he loves you fellas."

Robert nodded his head and commented, "Yeah but he's probably gonna spend all his time fishin' and kissin' his wife.

The boys began to laugh.

"That's right! Fishin' and kissin.'" Waynie said. "Mr. Davidson, fishin' and kissin' all day long."

Scotty added, "Yep, fishin' and kissin'."

J.T. smiled and nodded while pointing his finger at Scotty.

Giving a heavy sigh, Esther brought the table under a semblance of order. "Okay boys. Now remember you promised to be gentlemen tonight. Let's just be happy for Mr. Davidson. He's earned some rest."

Dinner was served buffet style and the young men enjoyed plates full of burgers, fries, boneless chicken, and several side choices. They did not overlook the dessert table as each of them had a *sweet tooth* and usually saw dinner as a meal that was in the way of what they really wanted.

Several speeches were made honoring the retiree and the nodding of heads showed the agreement of the crowd. After dinner and the program Esther and the gang made their way up to the head table to congratulate their friend. They were seated to the side, but close to the stage so the greeting line in front of them was not very long. This was a relief to Esther because she knew how impatient her men could be. She kept an arm around Scotty and tried to distract him as he bounced in the line.

Giving him a hug, Esther said, "We're sure gonna miss you Mr. Davidson. You really looked after me and my boys."

Nodding toward the boys, Mr. Davidson said, "These young men are going to be fine. As long as they have you to look after them, they'll be in great shape."

Waynie grabbed Mr. Davidson's hand and gave it a firm shake. "Mr. Davidson, you come see us. You come see us. You're welcome in our house. You're always welcome in our house. You come over and see us. We'll eat ice cream and have a groovy time. Gonna have a really groovy time."

"I sure will boys. You can count on it."

And true to his word, Mr. Davidson did stop by occasionally. He never stayed long, just long enough to greet each of the young men and let them know he was thinking about them.

Scotty stepped up, shook Mr. Davidson's hand, and said, "Good man, Mr. D. You're a good man."

J.T. was next. He shoved his hand forward and gave Mr. D. a hearty handshake while at the same time, bobbing his head and bending back and forth at the waist.

When Robert's turn came, he brought out his Gomer Pyle voice and said, "Gooollie Mr. D. Sure are gonna miss seein' ya."

With a smile of recognition, he said, "Thank you so much fellas! I'm gonna miss you guys too! But we'll keep in touch. I won't be hard to find."

Then as an elderly woman approached him, he turned to speak to her saying, "Excuse me boys."

When the appropriate time came, Esther led the boys out of the banquet hall and toward the exit. It had been a great evening and she was proud of how her young men carried themselves. As they headed toward the door, she noticed Waynie and Scotty greeting and shaking everyone's hands as they went by. She heard a couple of the boys' comments, and it brought a smile to her face.

"Nice to see you."

"You look good tonight!"

"Glad you could make it!"

"Come again soon!"

Those gathered responded well to the boys' comments with some stopping to ask their names. They even received a hug or two from some of the ladies.

As she watched them, Esther thought, "Well those two are not backward about being forward!"

Making their way through the parking lot Waynie called out, "Ms. Esther, we have money. Can we stop by Big Ray's on our way home. We've been good all night. All night we've been good." Big Ray's was an ice cream shop and it had grown to be the boys' favorite. They became big fans of Ray, and the man returned the favor. They never noticed it, but whatever they ordered somehow grew to be the next larger size.

Without turning around, she replied, "Not tonight gentlemen. It's late and the place is probably closed, Besides, it's a work night. You can't stay up late and expect to do a good job in the morning. And there's no point in beggin' to go somewhere else, 'cause you know what I'm gonna say."

Robert was quick to jump in, "You can't soar with the eagles in the mornin' if you're hootin' with the owls at night!"

"No hootin' goin' on tonight." Waynie added shaking his head. "That's for sure. No hootin' for us."

"That's right. No hootin' tonight" Esther said smiling.

Arriving home, Esther eased the van to a stop. The single-story house was a modest one with a small porch in the front and a bigger one on the side. Inside, the floor plan was an open one with the kitchen spilling into the living room unimpeded. A wooden stand supported a good-sized television with a DVD player on the shelf below. Behind the T.V. dozens of movies were neatly seated on the two built in shelves on the wall. The room held a well-worn couch, overstuffed chair, and a side table with a cushioned wooden chair. Down the hall were three bedrooms and two bathrooms.

Scotty and J.T. shared one room while Waynie and Robert shared the other. Both rooms were equipped with bunk beds, a matching pair of desks, and a single dresser the roommates shared. Esther's room was at the end of the hall. It was a bit smaller but had a double bed in it and a separate bath. The room was nicely decorated with a few paintings on the walls and a large dresser. Atop the dresser were several pictures: her sister, her mom and dad, the young men in her charge, two cousins, and her late husband.

Esther opened the front door simultaneously slipping off her jacket while she placed her pocketbook and keys on the table by the door. The young men piled in behind her.

"Now you fellas brush your teeth and get ready for bed. I'll be in in a few minutes to pray with you. It's been a good day and what do we do when we've had a good day?"

"We thank God for the day we had" The three talkers recited together.

"And what do we do when we've had a bad day?" she asked.

The men responded, "We thank God for getting' us through it and for givin' us another day tomorrow."

"That's right! Now let's get movin'. It's gonna be a good day tomorrow. I can feel it."

Waynie jumped in. "Good day tomorrow. Good day tomorrow." Then after looking down at this jacket, he remarked, "I'm gonna sleep in my suit."

Shaking her head, Esther gently rebuffed, "Oh no you aint. Now you boys remember to hang up your clothes. You'll need 'em again for church on Sunday."

Waynie and Scotty nodded, and all four men sauntered down the hall to their rooms.

After brushing their teeth and putting on their pajamas, the boys gathered in Waynie and Robert's room as they did every night. Waynie and Robert sat on the edge of the bottom bunk while Scotty and J.T. sat on the floor and leaned against the bed. Esther entered the room and sat on a chair by one of the desks.

She began, "We sure did have a good time tonight, didn't we?"

All the men nodded, and Robert added, "It was fun to dress up and go there."

Waynie said, "And I like the food. The food was good."

J.T. nodded and patted his stomach while pointing his other hand at Waynie.

"We should do that again," Scotty suggested.

Esther smiled, "Well, we can do something like that again someday, but that's the only time Mr. D is gonna retire. I'm sure there will be other times when we can dress up and go out to eat."

"Yeah, some other time," Waynie offered.

The other boys nodded their heads in agreement.

Esther nodded and said, "Well now it's time to get some rest. Maybe we'll all dream about what a good time we had." Then Esther leaned forward, folded her hands, and rested her elbows on her knees. On cue the boys folded their hands and bowed their heads.

She prayed, "Thank you Lord for the good day we've had. Thank you for Mr. Davidson. He's been so good to us. Please bless him in his retirement. Thank you for Waynie, Scotty, Robert, and J.T. Please protect us and bless all of us with a good night's rest. Amen"

In unison the boys repeated, "Amen."

With that, Esther stood up and the two boys walked out heading for their room. Esther stepped out of the door and turned toward Waynie and Robert saying, "Good night my friends!"

The boys followed with, "Good night Ms. Esther."

Before J.T. and Scotty entered their room, they turned to Esther for her good-night smile. She grinned broadly at them and said, "Good night my friends. Sleep well."

Scotty said, "Good night." J.T. nodded and patted his chest as he did each night.

In the hall as was her usual custom, Esther paused and whispered her own prayer. "Thank you, Lord for each of dem boys. They're good and kind and bring such meanin' to my life. They never asked to be this way, but they make the best of what they are. Please let them wake up refreshed and ready for a good day tomorrow. Thank you, Jesus! Amen!"

-6-
ANNIE

That Friday morning Esther rapped gently on each of the boys' rooms. "Time to get up!" As was her usual custom she quoted a Bible verse. "This is the day the Lord has made. We will rejoice and be glad in it." At other times she would say, "Good morning! His promises are new every morning." On more than one occasion she said, "The Lord is your shepherd. It's time for you sheep to get movin'." The young men usually responded by saying, "We're up," or "Yes, Ma'am."

When the boys emerged from the hall they were fully dressed and found breakfast almost ready. Esther knew the importance of a good breakfast and was always ready to stifle their hunger. Her breakfasts varied from pancakes to french toast, to home-made oatmeal. She made grits, eggs (scrambled or poached), or waffles. Esther knew what the group enjoyed and always prepared it just the way they liked it. There was always a few pieces of bacon, sausage, or cornbread to go along with the meal.

With breakfast completed, all four boys headed for the bus stop. Bus G-9 would drop them off just 100 yards from the shop where they all worked. When they first moved in together Esther would drive them to work in the house van. But the boys had heard of other guys at work taking the bus and wanted to experience it themselves. It turned out that they loved the adventure. She purchased bus passes for each of them and riding the bus to work became part of their routine.

At first, she would walk them the few hundred yards to the bus stop, but after a while they indicated that they felt comfortable walking alone and assured her that they knew the way. She even joined them for their first trip on the bus and felt better when the driver indicated that he would look after the guys. The first couple of times that they were *on their own*, she secretly followed them until she saw that they made it to the bus stop. After a few trips, she felt comfortable in letting them travel down the street and return home by the same route.

Esther had strict rules about their travel. They were always to stick together. They were neither to stop and talk to anyone, or even pause to pet a dog or cat. They were to stay on the sidewalk and only cross the street at the corner after each of them had looked both ways. And they were to go directly to the bus stop and come straight home from work on the same path they always took. She made each of the boys repeat the rules easing her mind about their freedom. Even J.T. had to communicate that he understood the rules. This was done by her asking him yes and no questions.

Even though her mind was eased regarding their trip to and from work, she still walked them from the house to the sidewalk and watched them as they crossed the street at the corner. If the weather was bad, she would drive them but for the most part the boys handled the trip on their own.

Each had a backpack and wore their favorite ball caps and sneakers. They moved at a fairly swift pace chatting randomly along the way.

They never seemed to focus on any particular subject. Their conversations bounced around everything from last night's dinner to a new car in someone's driveway. Each young man felt compelled to comment on whatever the passing topic would be and often one point of interest would simply develop into another.

"That mailbox door is open!" Waynie said pointing across the street. "Wide open!"

"I hope they don't lose their mail," Robert added.

Scotty reasoned, "Maybe the wind blew it open. It was really windy yesterday."

As if to take a cue, Robert began to quietly sing, "Yesterday, all my troubles seemed so far away…."

"I like that song," Scotty said. "Is that from the Beatles?"

Before Robert could answer, Waynie jumped in, "Beatles can't hurt you. Ms. Esther said so. They don't bite. They just fly around until they get tired. Then they rest. They gotta have some rest."

"I like to rest too!" Robert admitted. When I get tired, I like to rest."

"Look, that car has a flat tire," Scotty commented pointing in the driveway as they walked by.

And that was so often how their conversations went as they made their way to the bus stop.

Standing in line was Annie Foster. She was an attractive woman of twenty-six years who worked as a para-legal for the Jordan law firm on the other side of the city. Her long brunette hair was pulled into a bun behind her head. Her pocketbook and book bag rested against her leg and her hands held her traditional cup of hot coffee.

Minutes earlier, she had noticed a man standing in front of her at the coffee shop across the street. He was a slender man with dark hair, a goatee, and was about her age. When he got his coffee and turned around, he spotted Annie. Looking her up and down he said, "Well, good morning!" Annie brushed the side of her face with her left hand displaying her engagement ring and responded with a non-committal, "Mornin'."

When she got in line at the bus stop, the man stood directly behind her. Looking at his watch he commented to Annie, "My bus came early, this one's late. I never take this bus. Gonna be a great day. I can tell."

Annie turned her head to the side and gave a slight smile followed by a nod and a sip from the coffee cup she held in both hands.

The voices of Esther's young men arrived before they did. Annie watched them as they made their way noisily down the sidewalk. The man behind Annie gazed in the direction of the four men as they came their way. Turning his head to the man behind him he said, "Well here they come, the town geniuses. I thought they would be taking the short bus. Yep, gonna be a great day."

Hearing this Annie turned her head toward him. "Those are my friends. And each one of them is a great guy. Besides, shouldn't you be worried about your bladder problem?"

"What?" What bladder problem?"

With that Annie turned the rest of the way around, gave a slight grin and in one move splashed his light-colored pants with the last quarter inch of her coffee.

The man jumped out of line and wiped the coffee from his slacks with his bare hand. "Hey! Are you crazy?"

Without responding, Annie turned her attention to her four friends.

The boys crossed the street just as the bus was in sight. They picked up their pace when they caught sight of Annie.

"Annie! Annie!" They yelled. "Good morning! Good morning!"

"Good morning fellas! Good to see you!"

Annie stepped out of line and gave a *high five* to each of the young men.

Completing their normal ritual, the group of five filed onto the bus saying good morning to the driver with whom they had become familiar. They took their seats a couple of rows behind the coffee-stained man.

Waynie was seated next to Annie. He nudged her with his elbow and nodded in the direction of the man a few seats in front of them. He had noticed the man's stained pants and showed his recognition by the drop in his jaw. He quietly remarked, "That man up there wet his pants. Yup, he wet his pants. They'll probably laugh at him at work. I feel sorry for him. Sorry for him."

Annie gave more than a slight smile. "I think he'll be all right." Then turning to the others, she said, "Did you boys have a good time at the banquet last night?"

Robert spoke up, "Yeah, we did. We got dressed up in our Sunday clothes. Lots of food. Mr. Davidson's goin' fishin' and kissin' and kissin' and fishin.'"

Annie giggled a bit and said, "Well, I'm not sure what that means but I'm sure he'll be having a great time. You guys really liked him, didn't you?"

As usual, Waynie spoke for the group. "He is a good guy. Ms. Esther says we're getting' a new guy. Gotta break him in. Yup, gotta break him in. Whole lotta breakin' goin' on."

"He got retired" Scotty interjected as he bounced both legs and gave a few squeezes to his soft ball.

"We ate a lot of food," Robert added. "It was goooood!"

"Sounds like a lot of fun," Annie remarked.

"Oh yeah," Waynie added. "We listened to people talk. They really like Mr. D. He's a good guy!"

J.T. rocked back and forth nodding his approval at all the comments.

The rest of the ride was filled with small talk as the boys made comments about random sights that caught their eye. Robert spotted an elderly woman walking her small dog down the street. Like its owner, it had white curly hair. It trotted along rapidly moving its tiny legs. "Look! Look at that dog!" Robert declared. "I like that kind of a dog. He's small and pretty. I wanna get a dog someday."

"Ms. Esther said no dogs." Waynie added. "Got enough mouths to feed in the house."

Robert nodded in understanding. "But I still want one."

With that comment the bus eased to a stop.

"This is you guys, Annie announced. "Have a good day fellas."

As the men began to stroll out, Scotty turned to Annie and called out, "Have a good day, Annie! We'll see you at our house tonight."

She gave a thumbs up agreeing, "Yup! See you guys tonight!"

Waynie stood up and climbed passed Annie, "Ms. Esther's cookin' big. Ms. Esther's cookin' really big!"

"See you tonight boys!"

To Annie's surprise, Waynie took a few steps forward and stopped by the man with the coffee stain. Leaning over he quietly and sincerely suggested, "You should try depends. It will help you." Without waiting for a response, he turned and made his way to the exit.

Annie's hand covered her smile and muffled her laughter.

-7-
MEN AT WORK

Moments later the young men entered their place of employment, *Gladstone's Shop*. It was a sheltered workshop and employed over a dozen mentally challenged adults. The place was large and neatly kept, but showed signs of aging and needed some updating. The workroom was filled with wooden picnic benches and the lighting was provided by bulbs suspended from a rain-stained ceiling. The tongue and groove flooring was warped in some places and care had to be taken not to trip on the rising strips of wood. Plans for improvement had been talked about but at this point, had not eclipsed the conversation stage.

The men had worked there since moving to the house and felt comfortable and at home. Along with other items they assembled, they busied themselves with attaching wooden wheels onto toy trucks and cars as well as plastic handles on baskets. With very little training, each of the boys had mastered the tools needed for the work and the procedure for assembly.

The workers came from different parts of the county and were mentally challenged in various ways. Two of the workers were deaf, and one of them had no legs. The most common disability was found in those with Down Syndrome.

The supervisors were kind and patient especially with the new hires, making assimilation into the work force easy and enjoyable. Music was quietly and constantly being played over the speakers and each morning a different worker's name was drawn who would choose the style of music that was to enhance their day. The music ranged from golden oldies, to classical, and several categories in between. Whatever type of music was chosen, the crew seemed to enjoy it and often could be seen moving to the beat as they moved to place the finished products on the shelves.

Of all the workers, Robert as expected, seemed to connect with the music the most. When a song came on that he was most familiar with and fond of, he often stepped away from his table and sang along with the performer. Most of the time, the entire room applauded at the conclusion. Robert always gave an exaggerated bow to his co-workers and blew kisses to the crowd that cheered loudly in his mind.

When it was time for lunch, one of the supervisors would shout above the music and the noise of the workers, "Lunchtime! Everybody grab your lunch." Simultaneously and without delay, each of the employees got up from his place, retrieved his lunch, and headed for the break room. The room was brightly decorated with prints of nature and pictures of the workers scattered about the walls. It was neatly kept with chairs and round tables spread about. Plastic glasses of sweet tea and water lined the table at the front of the room and the employees routinely sat in the places they regularly occupied.

A number was placed on the chalk board signifying the number of days the team had gone without anyone dropping their drink. The current number was twenty-nine. Each time the number reached fifty, everyone was rewarded with their choice of a chocolate treat. Over time, the staff knew how much of each type of chocolate to buy because they learned that with this group, there was very little variation in choices.

When the young men entered the break room, Robert and J.T. sat at a table with a couple of other workers, while Waynie and Scotty sat at another table by themselves. As they finished their meal, Scotty leaned across the table toward Waynie.

"Hey…I know something about you!"

Waynie looked up, "No you don't!"

"Yes, I do!

"No! You don't!"

"Yes, I do! You like Annie."

"So. What's wrong with that?"

"Nothing. I'm just saying that I know it."

Waynie tried to hide his smile proclaiming, "You know Annie's really smart. She's smarter than you or me or anybody she works with. She's one of the smartest girls in the world."

Scotty nodded in agreement, "I know. Ms. Ether told me that Annie's a paralegal. I bet you don't know what a paralegal is, do you?"

Waynie leaned toward Scotty and asked, "Do you? Do you know what one is?"

"No. But I know that you have to be real smart to be one."

Waynie agreed saying, "Yeah, and Annie's real smart."

Processing their conversation, Waynie said, "I think that a lawyer is a legal. And Annie's a paralegal. That means that she's smarter than two legals."

Scotty nodded in agreement. "Yeah, Annie's really smart.

A grin came to Waynie's face. He said, "And she's pretty too!"

Scotty's smile matched Waynie's. "Ohhhhh!" He followed this by making kissing sounds.

Waynie's smile left his face. "Stop it. You retard!"

Scotty's smile departed as well. "You're not supposed to call people that. I'm gonna tell Ms. Esther. Besides, you're a retard too." Then grabbing his lunch box and empty cup, he added,

"But you're a retard in loooooove!"

Waynie shook his head giving a heavy sigh as he stood up with his empty cup.

Then the shop supervisor stepped away from his table and announced, "Okay gang, time to get back to work."

After a six-hour day, it was time to head home. When the bus arrived at their stop, the young men bounced down the steps and gathered on the sidewalk before making their way back home.

Waynie turned and faced the group announcing, "Today was a good day, a good day. We had a really good day."

Scotty agreed, "Yup. We all had a good day. But tomorrow's gonna be a great day.

"Why tomorrow?" Robert asked.

"Cause tomorrow is pay day." Scotty answered.

Robert and Waynie both shouted, "Oooooh pay day!"

"Yup," Scotty continued. "Ms. Esther will pick up our money and maybe take us to town. 'Cause I'm gonna buy me somethin' with some of my money."

"Like what" Waynie asked. "Whatcha gonna buy?"

"Like I don't know. Maybe a t-shirt or some candy. I might even buy a new movie."

Robert skipped a few steps and added, "I'm gonna buy somethin' too!" I might get a new set of markers."

Scotty spoke above the others, "We should get something for Ms. Esther. We need to buy something for Ms. Esther. She's the queen of the house you know."

In an unscripted move, all of them stopped on the sidewalk and the three boys broke out in a song they often sang to the tune of *Happy Birthday to you*, "She's the queen...of the house. She's the queen... of the house...She's the queen...of the house. She's the queen...of the house." J.T. moved along in rhythm with them by bobbing his head. The song ended as quickly as it had started, and the men turned and continued their trek toward home.

Unbeknownst to the gang, an elderly man and his wife were seated on their front porch directly in line with the boys. They were reading magazines and drinking iced tea. They often watched the young men walk by and waved to them as they passed. When the young men saw them, they each waved back following it with a loud "Hello."

Today, when the boys stopped in front of them it drew their complete attention to the young men. Hearing the song brought great smiles to their faces. When the song ended the man stood to his feet while his wife remained seated, and both applauded loudly. The man leaned on the railing and yelled, "Good job men! Good job!"

Hearing this the four of them stopped and faced the couple bowing and waving. Then they simply turned and continue walking.

A few steps later and without any prompting, Robert broke out with the words, "Two, four, six, eight," then the other two picked it up, "Score before we graduate." The group really didn't have a clear understanding of the meaning of the cheer, they just liked it because it rhymed and was easy to follow.

Annie's fiancé Greg had been watching a college football game with the boys. He thought it would be fun to introduce the game to them giving them common ground on which to be excited. He tried to explain the rules to them, but their questions had outdistanced his patience. At one point, they noticed some of the fans chanting in unison and asked Greg about it. Abandoning the idea of enjoying the game together, he taught them that cheer. The young men grasped it immediately and every once in awhile they would default to it for no apparent reason. This day was one of them.

The completion of a couple of rounds of the cheer was followed by a few high fives while the men sauntered toward the house. A few steps later Scotty raised his finger in the air and shouted, "We're number one." The others pointed their fingers skyward and joined in immediately saying, "We're number one!" They repeated the phrase three more times and dropped it as fast as they had started it.

A few strides short of one hundred brought them to the front steps of the house where they scrambled in announcing their arrival.

Scotty and Robert called out, "Ms. Esther, we're home!

Waynie gave his usual, "Home again, Home again, Jiggety Jig!"

-8-
DINNER WITH ANNIE

At home that evening, the boys were lounging around the living room watching T.V. while Esther busied herself in the kitchen. The faint sound of the doorbell could be heard above the television. Waynie jumped up quickly and announced, "I'll get it!" He opened the door and found Annie there holding a plate of brownies. "Annie! Annie! Come in. Come into our house!"

Waynie took her coat and called to the others, "Hey guys. Annie's here."

Together the men looked up and one right after the other shouted, "Hi Annie!" J.T. waved and patted his chest.

Waynie placed her coat on the nearby rack and took the plate from her. "Come in. Come in Annie." Esther caught Waynie's eye and gave him a wink.

On the way to the kitchen, Waynie made a detour to the back of the couch and announced to the others, "Hey you guys! Annie made brownies. We love brownies and Annie made them. Brownies with the boys. Gonna have brownies with the boys tonight!"

Annie strode to the kitchen and the two ladies embraced. "Your timing is perfect'" Esther said. "Dinner is just about done."

"I'm sorry Greg couldn't make it tonight," Annie said. He had a couple of meetings at the school."

Esther patted Annie's shoulder smiling. "Well, we'll just have to take a raincheck and get him here some other time. In the meantime, we'll have an extra brownie in his honor." With that she lifted her chin and called out, "Wash up gentlemen! It's time to eat."

Scotty grabbed the remote and flipped the T.V. off.

All four boys scrambled down the hall and took their turns at the sink. Moments later everyone was seated about the large rectangle table with Esther placed at the head. The table was filled with what she had discovered as the favorites of the group. Fried chicken, green beans, salad, apple slices, and mashed potatoes bursting with gravy, were all part of the evening's menu. Oohs and aahs were emitted from the boys as Esther brought each dish to the table and announced its contents. The plates and bowls of food were passed around and everyone filled their plate, but no one began eating until everyone was served and Esther gave the green light.

When Esther was seated, she patted the arm of Scotty sitting next to her stating, "Scotty, I believe it's your turn to thank the Lord for providing again."

Scotty nodded and everyone folded their hands and bowed their heads.

Scotty cleared his throat and prayed "Dear Lord, thank you for the food again. Thank you that we're not hungry like other people. Thank you for Annie and Ms. Esther. Amen."

The entire table followed Scotty's "Amen" with their own. Then Ms. Esther said, "Okay, now let's eat."

Without prompting, the group simultaneously began eating. The boys showed their approval with plenty of "Mmmms" and other comments of appreciation.

Just as the meal was finishing up, Robert cried out, "Oh, oh, uh oh." With that, he placed his thumb on his forehead and turned to everyone at the table. Each man followed Robert's move and placed his thumb on his forehead. Annie gave a look of confusion and Esther gave a sigh and gently shook her head. The men joined together and said, "Oh Annie! Oh Annie!" J.T. kept his thumb in place and smiled while pointing at her with his other hand and nodding.

Annie put both hands on the table, leaned forward and with a puzzled look said, "What? What does that mean?"

Robert pointed at her and filled her in, "You didn't give the sign. You did it! Annie Fawted! Annie Fawted!"

The boys all pointed at Annie repeating Robert's words, "Annie Fawted! Annie Fawted!"

Esther taped the table sharply with the knuckles of her right hand. "Now boys, this is not how we treat our guests." The boys' thumbs quickly came down from their heads and they looked down fighting with the smiles that were forcing their way out.

"Annie, you'll have to excuse their crudeness. There are just some things that can only be explained as *maleness*."

Annie smiled and nodded and put her thumb to her forehead, "Gotta remember that one!"

Esther's knuckles gently tapped the table again. And everyone turned her way. "Well now, it's time for dessert. Since we have a special guest that brought a special dessert, we gotta have some special entertainment before we can enjoy the extra blessing. Tonight, the cost of dessert will be a rhythm and a joke or song."

Immediately both hands of each man found a place on either side of their plates.

Annie looked confused again, but without a pause Esther said, "Follow me fellas!"

Esther began tapping out a beat on the table. She stopped and the boys each repeated it in unison. She gave another rhythm and the men followed. The third beat was more complex, but the men followed her effortlessly. When they were done, Annie applauded while giving a broad smile. "That was awesome guys! You fellas are great!"

"Now it's time for a joke or song. Who's got one?" Esther asked.

Raising his hand, Scotty announced, "I got one! I got a joke!"

Esther turned to Scotty, "Alright! You're on. Whatcha got?"

Scotty asked, "How come dinosaurs can't talk?" Silence and confusion covered the table. "'Cause they're all dead." With the punchline Scotty popped the table with his hand and convulsed in laughter.

Waynie pointed at Scotty and said, "Ohhhh! I get it! Dead dinasaws can't talk 'cause they're dead. That's a good joke right there. A groovy joke. Scotty told a groovy joke."

Smiling, Esther announced, "Well, that qualifies as a joke, so both the dessert fees have been paid. I'll go get the brownies.

Scotty smiled, "Yes!"

As Esther turned and took a step toward the kitchen, Annie raised her hand and said, "I know a joke." This brought Esther back to the table and she sat down again smiling.

One right after another the men said, "Tell us Annie! Tell us your joke! Go ahead Annie! Tell us!"

Annie asked, "What has six legs and ten teeth?"

This question was followed by complete silence at the table. No one made a sound including Esther. They just looked at her with puzzled expressions on their faces.

Leaning forward Annie said, "The night shift at the Waffle House."

Silence and stares again covered the group. After a short pause, the punch line hit Esther and she gave a grin and a smile. Then she stood up and headed for the kitchen.

Annie seemed bewildered and said to the boys, "You get it? The three people working at the waffle house have two legs each and so that makes six legs, but they only have ten teeth between all of them."

More silence followed.

Finally, Robert muttered, "That's not a good joke Annie!"

Scotty followed his lead with, "Keep being a legal, Annie!"

Waynie chimed in, "We may not give you any dessert Annie."

Annie looked down, "No dessert? No brownies? But I love dessert! In fact, I love dessert so much that sometimes I eat dessert before I eat dinner." With that she pulled her napkin to her face and gave verbal signs of sobbing.

Waynie immediately leaned in and patted her arm. "Don't cry Annie. We didn't mean to hurt your feelings."

Robert offered, "You can have my dessert, Annie. Please don't cry."

From behind the counter, Esther smiled broadly as she watched Annie perform.

Annie lowered her napkin to reveal a big smile. "Gotcha!"

All together the men cried out, "Oh Annie! You were just kidding us! You fooled us. You got us that time Annie." J.T. rocked back in forth giving his sign of approval.

A few minutes later, the brownies were devoured and Waynie invited Annie to the side porch to sit on the swing. The swing may have been the item in the house that was in the best condition. It was given to them by the church they all attended. It was made of slatted oak boards and had a Bible verse inscribed on a brass plate and mounted in the center.

One weekday evening, six members from Trinity Community Church arrived and knocked on the groups' door. Esther opened the door and recognized them immediately.

Trinity Community Church was not a large church, nor was it a wealthy church. But they were constantly looking for ways to help others. During Christmas season there was a toy drive. At Thanksgiving, they hosted a large dinner for the less fortunate. Every year, before school started, they supplied book bags for the children at the elementary school and they had it as part of their budget to support a state sponsored children's home. And now this! A wonderful gift for Esther and the boys!

"Oh, hi! How are you? Please come in!"

The six entered the house and the boys got up from the living room and came to greet them as well.

"Good to see ya' Pilgrims!" Robert said in his John Wayne voice.

"We're just watchin' some T.V." Scotty said. "You can watch it with us if you want."

Mr. Wells, a large black man with a deep voice, spoke for the group, "Thank you, but we just came over to bring you a gift. The people at church got together and thought we'd give you folks something special. It's a *Just Because* kind of gift. No special occasion. Just because we're friends."

Robert often tried to imitate Mr. Wells' deep voice, even at church but failed miserably. And that evening was no exception. When he said, "Good to see you Mr. Wells," it made the whole group laugh.

"You're gettin' better Robert. Keep practicing," the man suggested.

"Well, that's awfully nice of you folks, but you didn't have to give us anything," Esther exclaimed.

"We know," Mr. Wells explained, "but we wanted to get you something anyway."

The rest of the group was beaming and visibly anxious to give them their gift.

Finally, a woman in the back of the group spoke up. "Well come outside and check it out." They led Esther and the boys outside and directed their attention to the back of the truck. The tailgate of the truck was open and lying flat, exposing a brand-new porch swing.

The boys cheered and Ms. Esther's eyes filled with tears. "That's beautiful! Thank you! Thank you so much!" she choked. Then gathering her voice and turning to the young men, she said, "Will you take a look at this, boys. A new porch swing! Now we can have a good time sitting outside swinging."

The boys jumped up and down clapping their hands and exchanging high fives.

Then Esther noticed the engraved brass plate on the back rest of the swing. Pointing to it she read the words out loud, "...There is a friend who sticks closer than a brother. Prov. 18:24" Esther's eyes teared up again and she took a moment to gather her voice. "Wow! I can't tell you how thankful we are for all of you. You really are a blessing to us."

"Well, all of you are a blessing to us," one of the ladies said.

"Boys, what do you have to say to our friends?" Esther asked.

Waynie answered, "Thank you! Thank you so much!

Scotty added, "I like it. I like to swing!"

Robert pulled up his Gomer Pyle voice and simply said, "Shazaam!"

J.T. rocked up on his toes, smiled broadly, and popped the back of the truck a couple of times.

Two of the men carried the swing while J.T. and Waynie escorted them to the side porch. They set it down and both boys found a spot on it while it rested flat on the floor.

At the truck, Mr. Wells said, "Tom Moore will come by this week and put it up, In the meantime, think about where you want it and he'll take care of everything else."

"We sure will!" And thank you all so much! This is a wonderful gift isn't it boys?"

The young men in the driveway responded, "Yes, Ma'am! It's a wonderful gift! Thank you so much!"

With that, two men climbed in the truck while the others jumped in the car. Moments later they were out of sight and Esther was standing with all four boys in the driveway.

"Boy we have a great church," Esther exclaimed. "And they sure do love you guys."

"Yeah, they love us," Waynie agreed. "They love us like we're family."

Esther smiled, "That's 'cause in a way, we are family."

"Yeah! We're family." Robert exclaimed loudly.

Everyone in the house enjoyed this gift and spent a good bit of time sitting and gently swinging on it. Perhaps the swing was employed and enjoyed most by Esther. If the weather permitted, and after the men headed to work, she would often be seen with a cup of coffee and her Bible relishing the fellowship with both. It was not uncommon to hear her singing softly as she swayed back and forth. Esther had a sweet voice, and the men often heard her singing as she prepared a meal or straightened up the house. They would often join her as she sat at the piano and led them in a chorus or two.

It was common for J.T. to slide in next to Esther and jump in on some of the songs she was playing. It was just as common for J.T. to take over the music duties sweeping them into a different direction as the songs in his head parted from those in Esther's.

Esther found that music was a unifying exercise and she always played simple tunes making it easy for the men to follow. When she called them to the piano, they picked up on her lead and had no trouble joining in. Many times, she would say the words to the chorus and have them repeat them. Then she would introduce the tune and ask them to join in.

In time, they learned songs such as, "Today is mine and I'm feelin' fine. I know I'm blessed all the time." And "I've got the joy, joy, joy, joy down in my heart...Where? Down in my heart. Where? Down in my heart...I've got the joy, joy, joy, joy down in my heart. Down in my heart to stay." Invariably, one of the boys would request his favorite and of course, Esther would smile and comply.

When birthdays came passersby could easily hear the piano and voices loudly singing *Happy Birthday*. Despite their mental short comings, the music and singing always seemed to light up the entire house and bring a sense of peace and happiness.

That evening, when Annie and Waynie sat down on the swing, they talked about how nice it felt outside and how good dinner was. The television could be heard from inside and the night creatures from outside.

With noticeable nervousness, Waynie turned to Annie and asked, "Annie, can I ask you a question?"

Annie answered, "That is a question."

This caused a pause in Waynie's voice as he processed her answer and realized she was right.

"But that's not the question I wanted to ask. Can I ask you another question?"

Nodding and smiling, Annie said, "Sure."

"Can I be your boyfriend so you can be my girlfriend?"

"Oh, Waynie! That is so sweet of you! You are such a special young man. But I'm afraid I can't. You see, I have a fiancé. You know Greg. He's my fiancé."

"I know. But I was thinking that he could be your fiancé and I could be your boyfriend."

"Well, Waynie, I'm afraid that it doesn't work that way. You see, relationships go along on different levels. First, boys and girls are friends. Like you and me. Then they become boyfriend and girlfriend. Then they get engaged to be married, so they're fiancés. Then they get married and are husband and wife. You're not supposed to have a fiancé and a boyfriend. Do you understand?"

"But I wanted us to be boyfriend and girlfriend."

"I'm afraid we can't. But I'll tell you what, and this is almost as close. I'm a girl and I can be your friend. And you're a boy, and you can be my friend. That's kinda close."

Waynie looked down not attempting to hide his disappointment. "Okay."

Annie extended her right hand with her little finger outstretched. "You gotta pinky swear that you'll always be my friend. That's what friends do."

Waynie raised his right hand to meet hers. "Okay. I promise."

They were just about to join hands when he said, "Wait!" With that he touched his pinky finger to his tongue. "This makes it 'ficial."

Annie followed his lead. "Okay. Now it's 'ficial."

The two joined fingers in the 'ficial declaration and smiled.

Annie changed the moment by saying, "Let's go inside and see what the others are doing."

The two of them left the swing and headed for the side door. Just before the door Waynie nudged Annie's shoulder and asked, "Annie, would you do me a big favor, a really big favor?"

"Sure Waynie. What is it?"

"When we go in the house, can I hold your hand? Just for a minute. You don't have to hold mine, I just want to hold yours."

Annie looked over his shoulder. She could see Esther at the kitchen sink and the others sprawled out on the couch and floor in front of the television.

Annie gave Waynie a smile and extended her hand. "Sure, my friend."

The two entered the house holding hands. The three boys in the living room noticed them and smiled. Esther and Annie's eyes met, and both shared a nod and grin. Waynie joined the boys while Annie made her way to the kitchen. The noise of the television concealed their conversation as Annie slipped around the counter and stood next to Esther.

"He's a tender young man" she said as she grabbed a towel and joined Esther in drying the dishes.

"Yes. They all are. But I think maybe Waynie's a little more tender than the others. He doesn't make any effort to hide his feelings or voice his opinion."

"I work with some people like that, but there's no tenderness connected to them."

Esther gave a nod and a small chuckle, "I think we all know people like that."

The ladies continued their talk as they finished taking care of the dishes.

Shortly after Annie left, Esther made her way down the hall to Waynie's room. Annie had shared with her their conversation, and Esther could sense that he was digesting it. She knew she would find him on his bed because that's where he often went to process things.

A year ago, as they were eating lunch at a table in the park, three middle school kids cruised by on their bikes. As they passed her men, she heard them make several derogatory comments. This didn't seem to bother the others, but she noticed that Waynie's countenance fell. He became quiet and less engaging the rest of the day.

Just a few months ago, she was with her fellows at *Big Ray's* ice cream bar. Two young boys came in with their moms. They looked to be about six years old. On seeing the boys seated at a table enjoying their treats, one boy turned to the other and said, "Those guys are retards. My dad told me to stay away from them." The others acted as if they didn't hear that comment, but Waynie heard it and it pierced him to the heart.

Each time she visited with him in his room, she was able to talk him back into being the Waynie she knew and loved. When she entered the room that night, she found him lying on his side on the lower bunk with his face to the wall.

Esther sat on the edge of the bed and tapped his shoulder. Waynie didn't move. She knew he was fighting to keep his emotions inside. This was a rare situation in which he did that.

Quietly Esther asked, "Annie told me you two talked tonight. You wanna tell me 'bout it?"

She heard him sniffle and saw him nod his head.

Esther continued, "Waynie, I'm sorry you're hurting. But I can promise you this. As time goes by, you'll hurt less and less. You are a terrific young man, and you have lots of friends. Everyone likes you because you have such a great heart. You're caring and loving and giving. That's why you're so special. You do have a wonderful heart."

Waynie turned to her, "Ms. Esther?"

"Yes, honey?"

"I know I don't have a grown-up mind. But I have a grown-up body and a grown-up heart. I wish I could trade my grown-up heart for a grown-up mind. Maybe then I would understand. Maybe then it wouldn't hurt so much."

Esther patted his shoulder. "Maybe so. But we don't get to choose how God made us. Our job is just to make the best out of what we are. And do you know what?"

"What?"

"I don't know anybody who's doing a better job at that than you."

Esther shook his shoulder and stood to exit. "Tomorrow's gonna be a better day. You'll see."

Waynie nodded and gave a faint smile as Esther exited.

-9-
MR. DRYDEN

Early Monday afternoon Esther was in the kitchen wearing her apron, prepping for dinner, and waiting for her men to come home from work. This evening, they would be enjoying burgers, baked potatoes, and salad. The doorbell rang and she pulled her apron off and quickly rinsed her hands before heading for the door. She was expecting Mr. Dryden from social services and was confident that he had arrived. She peered through the glass door and saw a man wearing a jacket without a tie and carrying a folder. Mr. Dryden was a middle-aged man, slender but not skinny. His face displayed a kind demeanor and carried a mustache that ran down into a small and neatly trimmed beard.

As Esther opened the door she said, "You must be Mr. Dryden. They told me you'd be here today. Come in! Come in!"

"Yes, Ma'am. And you must be Ms. Snyder."

"Please call me Esther."

He entered the home while shifting the folder to his other hand. Esther escorted him into the living room and motioned him to a chair with her hand. When he was seated, she said, "Can I get you something to drink Mr. Dryden?"

"No. No thank you I'm good. And please call me Mark."

Sitting down on the edge of the couch Esther said, "Okay Mark. Well, it didn't take them too long to replace Mr. Davidson. He was a wonderful man, and the boys really took to him. I'm sure they'll enjoy getting to know you as well."

"I hope so. I've only been doing this for four years. But I'm enjoying it. They transferred me here from the other side of the county so I'm still learning my way around."

"I'm sure you figure it all out quick enough."

Turning to Esther, Mark opened the folder. "I've heard a lot of good things about what you're doing with the boys. It says here that you have four young men living with you."

"That's right. We've been together for over two years now. They're really doing well."

Mark tapped the folder, "That's what the report says. How are the men doing at work?"

"They're doing just fine. I could drive them to work but they said they wanted to try the bus. And they've been riding the bus ever since their first trip. The bus drops them off really close to the sheltered workshop and I think it gives them a sense of independence and maturity. Besides, they like being around other people."

"Are you ever concerned that they may not be safe?"

"Not at all," she answered shaking her head while looking down. "The bus driver and everybody on the bus look after them. I can see them walking all the way down the street almost all the way to the bus stop. And so far, they've never broken one of my *bus rules.*"

"Bus rules? What are the bus rules?"

"Well," Esther began holding her fingers up while counting out the rules. "One-they gotta stick together. No one runs ahead and no one lags behind. Two-they are not to stop. Three-they gotta stay on the sidewalk until they get to the corner and have to cross the street. Four-they only cross after all four of them look both ways. And lastly," she said holding up her fifth finger, "They are to go straight to the bus stop and come straight home after work. No detours."

"Sounds like good rules," Mark said, "Sounds easy enough to follow".

"I think so."

"Do you think they have a clear concept of money?"

"Well, I don't know what you mean by a clear concept, but they know that they get paid for the work they do. We go down and pick up their paychecks on Saturdays twice a month and then head to the bank. Each of the men has his own savings account. They also know that it cost money to buy things. They don't know the difference between a thousand dollars and a billion dollars, but they understand money in more simpler terms."

"Like what?"

"Well, they know that they have more than some and less than others. They know they don't make enough to live off of, but they understand that they can use their money to help other people live better. Come into the kitchen and I'll show you what I mean."

Esther led Mark into the kitchen area. With her foot, she slid the short metal step in front of the fridge and opened the upper cabinet. Reaching in, she pulled out a tin can covered with pictures of goats, pigs, chickens, and a cow. She put the can on the counter and opened it up revealing several single and five-dollar bills.

"This is what we call the *blessing can*. About a year and a half ago, we were watching television and learned about some people in Sudan that weren't doing well and needed some help. The program outlined what they needed and how people could help them. The boys decided that they would pitch in and do something. So, they sent away for a packet of information and when it came, they jumped right in."

Mark nodded in understanding and tipped his head to the side in surprise.

"A couple times each month, they put a little money into the *blessing can*. When they have enough, they send it in with the instructions to buy the items they can afford for a village. These are the pictures of what they've bought so far."

Esther pulled our several pictures and spread them out on the counter. Mark's face showed how impressed he was.

"So far, they gave enough money to buy a couple dozen chickens, four goats, and two pigs."

Then holding up a picture of a cow she said, "And this is what they're planning on buying next. They even named the cow *Bertha* and can't wait to send her to a village. And every two weeks they want a report from me on how close they are to buying *Bertha*. They're constantly talking about how great it will be to provide milk for the people."

Mark picked up the picture of the cow. "This is amazing! I can't tell you how impressive it is."

"Those fellas get so excited every time they have enough to make a purchase. And every time they reach their goal, the five of us host a 'bless your socks off party.'"

"What's that party like?"

"Well, not including Annie and Greg, they each get to invite a friend. It always seems to be the same friend from work or church.

"Who's Annie and Greg?"

"Oh, I didn't tell you about them," she said putting her hands on her hips. "They're a couple of folks who became friends with the boys just after we moved in here. They met Annie at the bus stop and she introduced them to Greg. Annie works in town as a paralegal, and

Greg is a P.E. teacher at the high school. They're engaged. The fellas have sort of adopted them and they've become good friends."

"I see," Mark said with a slight nod of his head.

Well, for our party, we all get together here on a Friday or Saturday night, and we have music, and food, and laughter and singing. And the house is decorated with pictures of whatever they were able to buy for the village. It's a great time."

Mark's eyebrows rose to their fullest extent. "Wow! This whole thing is really something!"

"I think so, Esther affirmed. "So in answer to your question about them understanding money, I don't know if they fully get it or not, but they know enough to spend some, save some, and give some away."

Mark nodded and said, "I wish more people knew that."

Esther's nod matched Mark's. "Sure enough. You see, generosity is a character trait. And character traits are like vegetables in the garden. You've got to water them and nourish them if you want them to grow. But once they grow, they can help nourish a lot of people. And those boys have learned that it really is a bigger blessing to give than to receive."

"You couldn't be more right Ms. Esther."

"I'm really proud of those young men. They're not perfect, but they've come a long way," she said while smiling, looking up and gently shaking her head.

Their conversation was interrupted by the swinging of the front door and the voices of all four young men with Scotty announcing their arrival. "We're home Ms. Esther. Big day for us!"

Waynie jumped in, "Another day, another dollar! Another dollar for another day."

J.T. raised both fists as he joined the celebration.

Their entry brought a smile to the face of Esther. "Hello boys! Come here! I want you to meet someone."

The young men immediately gathered around Ms. Esther. "Gentlemen, this is Mr. Mark Dryden. You can call him Mr. Mark, or Mr. D. Do you remember Mr. Davidson?"

The men all nodded.

"Well, Mr. Dryden has taken his place. He's gonna do for us what Mr. Davidson did and he's gonna be the same kind of friend that Mr. Davidson was.

The men all nodded in understanding.

Then Esther introduced each young man to their guest. As she introduced them, they stepped forward and shook his hand.

Mr. D, "This is Waynie."

While holding his hand Waynie chanted, "It's good to meet you Mr. D. Real good to meet you! Real good!"

Pointing to Robert she said, "And here is Robert."

Before Robert shook his hand, Waynie jumped in. "Ms. Esther, he's not Robert right now. He's Elvis."

With that introduction Robert stepped forward, wiggled his left leg, swung his right arm around in a big circle and extended it toward their guest. In a voice surprisingly similar to Elvis', he said, "Thank you! Thank you very much."

Mark grinned widely and shook the icon's hand.

Patting Scotty on the back, Esther said, "And this is Scotty." Then turning to Scotty, she said, "Scotty, now stand still and shake Mr.

Mark's hand." Scotty stepped forward after stepping to both sides and shook his hand.

Without introduction and of course without a word, J.T. stepped forward, bowed at the waist, gave a closed mouth but wide smile and shook Mark's hand.

Then turning to the rest of the boys Esther said, "Now boys, Mr. D and I have got a few things to talk about. If you want some fruit, you can grab a piece, then I want you to head to your rooms for a while. I'll come get you when we're done."

With a few nods Waynie and Robert slipped around the counter grabbed a piece of fruit and joined the others who were already down the hall. Mark and Esther both smiled as they heard Waynie announce, "Fruit in our rooms. Gonna have fruit in our rooms. Nothing like fruit in our rooms."

"Let's go back to the living room," Esther suggested escorting Mark in that direction.

When they both were seated, Mark said, "Tell me about the incident with Waynie in the grocery store."

Rolling her eyes and gently shaking her head, Esther said, "Oh, that! That happened a little while after we moved in here. I'm surprised it's still in the file. Waynie worked down at Bailey's grocery store you know baggin' groceries and cleanin' up a little. He' a good worker and was doin' a real good job."

Mark nodded and added, "It says in the file that there was some sort of confrontation between Waynie and a customer."

"I'm not sure you'd call it a confrontation. Waynie was busy baggin' groceries when a woman came along with a small baby girl. Waynie looked at the baby and smiled. He asked her if that was her baby. She said, 'Yes her name's Olivia.' Then she said, 'Don't you think she's beautiful?' Well, Waynie is as honest as the day is long. He just looked at that baby and leaned into the woman and said, 'No, she's ugly.' Well, that woman had a hissy fit right there in the store."

"Mr. Bailey came over and tried to calm things down, but the hornets were already out of the nest. He had to let Waynie go. Two days later he was workin' with the other boys at the sheltered workshop. He's doin' fine and is just as happy there as anywhere I guess."

Mark nodded showing his satisfaction with her explanation. "How are the men getting along at work?"

"Well, they're doin' just fine. They catch the bus at 7:30 every morning and they get off close to the plant. They're never late and the boss says they're doin' a good job."

Mark gave a smile and said, "I see. Well, every report that Mr. Davidson filled out says you're doing a great job but I'm glad I got to hear from you myself."

"Well, the guys are down the hall. Would you like to check out their rooms?"

"Sure!"

Esther led Mark down the hallway to the bedrooms. The hall was lined with pictures of the young men. Mark moved slowly down the hall pausing several times in front of the many pictures. The men were seen in the park, at work, at the community pool, around the dinner table, and with several people Mark didn't recognize. It was clear to him that the young men were living a full life.

Near the end of the hall, Esther pointed toward the closed door to her bedroom. "That's where I stay," she said. Do you need to see that?"

"No. No need for that."

Across the hall was Scotty and J.T.'s room. Knocking while opening the door, Esther announced to Mark that this was Scotty and J.T.'s room. J.T. was lying on the bottom bunk, while Scotty was sitting at the desk doodling. J.T. swung his legs to the floor and sat up. Scotty spun on the chair so he would be facing his *guests*.

When Mark stepped in, he found a fairly neat room with two desks, a dresser, a bunk bed, and a closet. There were several pictures on the wall of people posing with each of the two boys. Mark guessed that these were family members. There were also two posters-one at the head of each bed. One poster was an aerial view of the Grand Canyon while the other was of a deer staring straight into the camera lens.

Both posters held significance to each of the boys. Scotty's poster of the deer held a memory of an adventure he had when he was twelve. On a sunny Saturday afternoon his parents had taken him to a petting zoo. Immediately Scotty found himself surrounded by several animals in the corral. He had a bag of oats which contributed greatly to his popularity among the wildlife. The oats were gone almost immediately but Scotty showed no signs of panic or despair. He just kept turning in a circle while petting each animal. And his parents kept taking pictures of Scotty while he was enjoying himself among his new friends.

There was a small deer that seemed particularly attached to Scotty. Though he had no more food, the animal stayed close by his side receiving plenty of pets and hugs from Scotty.

With one arm around the deer's neck and looking at his parents standing outside the corral, Scotty informed them, "His name's Duke!"

"Duke huh?" his dad asked.

"Yup. Duke the deer," the young man answered.

When it came time to leave, Scotty struggled over their departure.

Turning to his father and wrapping his arm around the neck of his new friend he asked, "Can I take Duke home with me? He really likes me."

"No son. He's gotta stay here. This is his home."

"But he can stay with us. He can have a new home with us."

"But son, if he comes home with us, then the other children who come here won't be able to enjoy him."

Scotty looked down as if he was working it all through his brain. He gave the little deer a hug and said, "Goodbye Duke! I'll come back and see ya sometime!" Then he joined his parents outside the pen.

Two days later, Scotty's mother Adele arrived home with a gift for Scotty. After dinner that night, and while they all were still seated at the table, she rose, reached into the closet, and pulled the gift out. It was a long tube in a plastic bag. Only Adele knew the contents.

"Well, Scotty, it's not your birthday," Adele said as she handed the gift across the table to him. "But I saw this and thought you would like it."

Scotty said, "Thank you," and pulled the tube from the bag. When he unrolled it, he found a poster of a deer looking straight at him. Immediately he exclaimed, "Duke! This is Duke!" and everyone at the table clapped while Scotty beamed.

And everyone in the house knew the poster at the head of Scotty's bed was a picture of his *close friend*, Duke.

J.T.'s poster held significance as well. When J.T. was about ten years old, his parents, Alex and Wendy had taken him to the Grand Canyon on vacation. It was not his first flight, but his obvious excitement in the plane made it seem like it was. He rocked back and forth the entire trip smiling and pumping his fist in the air. Those sitting by seemed to understand and several of them made encouraging comments as they walked by.

The family hiked, went on a boat ride in Lake Powell, ate beyond their comfort levels, and rode bikes along the rim of the canyon. But the highlight of the trip for all of them was their plane ride above the canyon. Alex and Wendy were uncertain how J.T. would react to being in a small plane, but after discussing it for a short time, decided to give it a try. So, they mounted the twelve-passenger craft and soon found themselves airborne. To their pleasant surprise, not only was J.T. unafraid, he was overflowing with excitement. They had purposely seated him at the window and from the moment he sat down, his eyes were glued to the view outside.

When they reached their peak altitude, the canyon came into view. It was all the two could do to keep their son from jumping out of the window. He kept alternating between staring out the window and grabbing Alex's arm and pulling him to look outside. Wendy laughed continually as she watched her son's excitement. He had been excited about other things in his life, but this joy was miles beyond anything they had witnessed.

When they landed, the three of them headed into the gift shop. Within minutes of entering, they found J.T. standing still and pointing at a poster of an aerial view of the canyon. He pointed with his right hand while pumping his fist out and up with his left. There was no choice but to buy the poster. And when J.T. moved into the house with the other guys, the poster moved in with him and was mounted almost immediately.

Moving to the next room, Esther said, "And this is Waynie and Robert's room. It may not be as neat as the other one."

She knocked and opened the door and Mark saw that she was correct. He stepped in and found the room to be a mirror image of the previous one including a poster at the head of each bed and pictures of the young men with people he again guessed were family. The floor held a couple of t-shirts, two or three picture books, some markers, and a single shoe. For some reason they never discovered, the other shoe was sitting on top of the desk.

Waynie was lying on the bottom bed with his headphones on his eyes closed, and his feet resting against the bed above. On his chest sat the core of an apple. Robert was leaning on the desk looking out the window. When they entered, Robert completed a mildly dramatic spin and said, "Come in, come into our room. This is the best room in the house."

Because of his headphones, Waynie didn't notice that the two had entered. But when Esther tapped him on the shoulder, he immediately sat up pulling the headphones off.

Waynie shouted, "Mr. D! Good to see ya! Good to see ya in our room!"

Just like the other room, at the head of each bed was a poster. The upper bunk had a poster of a man's feet on the high wire crossing a giant waterfall. Because Waynie was on the bottom bunk, Mark guessed that this one belonged to Robert. Robert had always been enamored by heights.

One fall day, all four sets of parents of the grown men decided it was a good idea to take the entire group out for a day of adventure. They wanted to give Esther some time off and they wound up at the circus. The clowns, the animals, the colors, and the various acts locked in the attention of the entire group. But Robert was completely enamored by the high wire act. While the other men held a nervous look, Robert kept staring and making comments. "Look at him!" he said. "He's way up there! He's good! I wish I could do that! He's really good!"

The others kept looking away and Scotty was biting on the end of his sweatshirt. But Robert never took his eyes off the performers above.

At one point, a woman stepped on the wire wearing a blindfold. "Ohhhh, look at her! She's good too!" Robert said. "She can't see. She can't see at all!"

The other three glanced and refused to look up again.

When the evening was over the group divided up and the boys got into the van with Waynie's parents while the other parents jumped into Alex and Wendy's van.

Over the next couple of visits that Robert's parents made, Robert brought up the talent of the tight rope performers.

"Those walkers up in the air were good! They were really good!" he would say. "I wanna do that someday."

When his parents showed up one day with the poster looking down at a man's feet on the high wire, it came as no surprise to anyone. And Robert was filled with excitement and couldn't wait to put the poster on the wall.

Waynie's poster showed Jesus surrounded by a group of children and, like the others, it was pinned to the wall at the head of his bed. Waynie's heart and mind became glued to the story of Jesus and the children. One Sunday morning, Pastor Corby was preaching about how Jesus welcomed the children and encouraged them to come to him holding them and blessing them.

When the service was over and people were greeting the Pastor and his wife, Viola, Waynie waited in line with Esther and the boys. He was clearly excited and couldn't wait to speak to the pastor. He wasn't speaking very loudly, but those around him could easily hear him repeating, "Jesus and the children. Jesus and the children."

When he got to the pastor, he shook his hand and said, "Good message! Good message! Jesus and the children. Good message pastor!" While shaking his right hand, the pastor placed his other hand on Waynie's shoulder and said, "Thank you Waynie! Glad to hear it." Then he looked Waynie in the eye and said, "Ya know, Waynie, if you had been there, Jesus would have held you close and blessed you too!"

Waynie had no Immediate response. He just nodded and looked down as if processing the scene. Esther thanked the pastor and gave Viola a hug.

On the way to the van, Waynie nudged Ms. Esther and said, "If I was there, Jesus would have held me close and blessed me too. That's what Pastor told me. Jesus would have blessed me too!"

The very next Sunday, at the conclusion of the service, Jim and Elizabeth Crowe came up to Waynie and the gang. They had been behind Esther and the boys in the greeting line the previous week and heard Waynie's comments. Elizabeth handed Waynie a rolled-up poster saying, "Good morning Waynie. Jim and I heard that you liked last week's message about Jesus and the children, and we wanted to give you this."

Waynie took the poster, and said, "Thank you." Esther helped him unroll it and when he saw the picture of Jesus with a child on his lap surrounded by other children, he said loud enough for everyone to hear, "Jesus and the children. That's Jesus and the children. Jesus blessing the children."

At the outcry, all eyes in the sanctuary turned in their direction and saw Waynie holding the poster and stomping his feet and hugging Elizabeth.

Glancing again at the room, Mark stated, "Very nice." He and Esther waved to the boys and exited. Esther led Mark back to the living room and the two sat down. Mark sat on the overstuffed chair while Esther settled into the couch.

After a short time of silence, Mark turned his head toward Esther and said, "Esther, I'm afraid I have to share some very bad news with you."

"Okay."

"This is really hard for me to say because we just met today. Every report we have on this home regarding you and the boys is a great one. You've done a fantastic job with those young men and what I've been instructed to share with you is no reflection on that. But the higher ups have reviewed the report the building inspectors gave last month and have made a decision about the house. You know there are some serious structural problems especially under both bathrooms. The roof needs to be re-done, and some foundation issues have to be addressed."

"I see."

"Well, the contractors say it will cost upwards of $50,000 to do all that work. Along with that, there is still $45,000 left on the mortgage. That's $95,000 that the state just doesn't have. And with what's happened to the budget and all, they're recommending that we close this house and relocate the young men. It's a matter of safety more than anything else."

Esther's face clearly showed her disappointment. Her brow furrowed as she said, "Well I'd gotten a letter from the state, but all it said was that some changes were coming. It didn't say they were planning on doing away with this house altogether."

I know. They assigned me the task of filling in the details. I'm sorry! I know this is not the news you expected."

"But this is where the boys live. This is their home. How can the state just take this from them? What's gonna happen to those fellas?"

"They'll be taken care of. They'll probably be able to keep their jobs and arrangements will be made for them to be housed in other units."

Esther leaned forward, "You mean they'll be separated? Doesn't the state know how hard it is for guys like them to adjust to change?"

Mark's forward lean matched Esther's, "Well nothing will happen right away of course. In fact, it will probably be a month or so. But I felt it fair to let you know in advance. And with the great reviews you've been given as their house mother, I'm sure a position will be secured for you as well."

Esther gently shook her head, "I'm not worried about me. I'm thinking about those young men. They're like brothers. They're family.

Tossing them in another home will devastate them. And they're doing so well here. You said it yourself."

"Ms. Esther, please try to understand. None of this is my choice. I don't make these decisions. I wish I had some say in it, but I'm just a part of the machine."

At this point, Esther was running out of patience and the ability to control her temper. She stood and said, "Well you just tell dem people, dem higher ups that the machine's broken. And don't nobody fix a machine by burning down the factory and losin' all the parts."

Mark stood up slowly and adjusted his folder, "I understand. And I agree with you. And I'm sorry. I'll be sure to tell those in the state office how you feel. I don't think it will matter, 'cause at that level everything comes down to the bottom line. But I will tell them."

Esther's voice and emotions softened a little, "Now I'm not blaming you Mr. D. But I know that common sense is not a common thing. And not one of dem people who make the rules is willing to come down here and play the game. And you can tell them I said that too!"

"Yes, Ma'am. You can be sure that I will."

Esther escorted him to the door. They wished each other well and Mark made his way down the steps toward his car. Esther's eyes followed him all the way to the car. She closed the door turned and leaned against it. Her eyes began to fill with tears, and she looked upward, "Lord, we need you. We need you in a big way."

-10-
SHARING THE NEWS

Three days later, while they all cleaned up after dinner, Esther told the men, "Boys, let's leave the dishes for a while. I want to talk to you about something. Come into the living room and sit down."

The four men left the kitchen and bounced into the living room. Waynie grabbed the cushioned chair while the other three plopped down on the couch. Esther pulled the chair from the side table and sat down.

Taking a deep breath, Esther began, "Fellas, I gotta tell you, you men have done a great job living and working with each other. You've become such a close family and I'm so proud of each of you! But sometimes things happen that you have no control over and no choice in. Mr. D is a really nice man and I'm sure he wrote some really good things about each of you and put it in his folder. But I just got a note today from his boss. You all know that our house is not in good shape. It needs a lot of work." The men nodded in agreement.

Holding up the letter Esther continued, "It seems that the house needs a lot more repairs than social services is willing to pay. So what they're planning on doing soon, but not right away, is finding a new home for you boys to live in. Now, you guys will all be fine. You'll still be able to work and earn money and you'll have a great home to live in too. You just might not be able to live together.

Waynie said, "What do you mean? What does that mean?"

"Well, it means that each of you might be in different houses from each other."

Scotty leaned forward and asked, "You mean we won't live together anymore?"

"I'm afraid so."

The boys' reactions were immediate.

J.T. began rocking back and forth and bouncing the fist of his right hand in the air and his left hand on the seat cushion. All those who knew him understood this to be his sign of great fear, frustration, or anger.

Scotty stood up and began pacing the floor.

Finally, Waynie asked, "You comin' with us Ms. Esther?"

"I'm not sure. It don't look like it."

Waynie stood up putting his hands on his hips, "Well, then I don't want to go. No Ms. Esther, No Waynie. We're like a team. Just like a team. We always stick together. Like a team. We're a family! A family team!"

Robert was chewing the heel of his hand. "I don't wanna go! I wanna stay here. I don't wanna go! Please don't make us go!" The tears began to form in his eyes.

Scotty stopped pacing behind the couch and put his hand on the back cushions, "We didn't do nuthin' wrong. We've been good guys. All the time, we've been good guys. Please Ms. Esther tell them we been good!"

Esther put her hands to the side of her face. Her voice was shaking, and she did her best to control her emotions, "Now, listen. Listen to me boys. Look at me. Look right at Ms. Esther."

Each of the young men stopped what they were doing and turned their eyes toward her.

"You fellas are the best thing that's ever happened to me. And you're the best thing that's happened to this town and this house. This has nothing to do with you being good, working hard, staying out of trouble, or loving the people you meet. It's just that this old house wasn't made to last forever. We've got to move out soon, but we'll all be fine. Ms. Esther will be fine and each of you will be fine, even if we're not together."

Waynie waved his hand but didn't wait to be called on, "I got money. I got a lot of money in the bank. I can go get it and we can fix up this house. I got lots of money."

Esther tilted her head and gave a slight grin showing her pity, "I'm afraid you don't have nearly enough. Now what we need to do is pray. We need to ask God to come to our rescue just like he rescued Moses, and Joshua, and Daniel, and Paul, and all the others. There is an answer and it's found in God."

Waynie shrugged his shoulders, "What about His cows?"

"What cows?"

"The ones on the hills."

"Oh. You mean, He owns the cattle on a thousand hills?"

"That's right! Maybe God can sell some cows and give us the money."

Scotty realized a plan was forming and said, "Maybe we can sell the milk!"

Esther nodded her head. Slipping off the chair and to her knees she said, "Well we'll just have to ask him won't we? Let's pray."

The three boys moved to their knees as well. Scotty came around the couch and joined the others. They clasped their hands and placed the back of their thumbs on their foreheads and gently tucked their chins to their chests.

Esther gave a slight smile at the sight of her young men bowed for prayer, "Father in heaven, we know we're your children and you care about us. We know that the sparrow doesn't fall without you knowing it. We know that you care about us more than the birds. But you know that we're in a bind again. The people in charge say that we gotta leave this place and that these boys may not be able to live together. We believe that you do all things well. Would you either change their minds or change our situation? This is our Red Sea, and we need you to part the waters for us Lord. Please Lord, we're asking you to show up and show off. We ask these things in Jesus' name, Amen."

The boys all repeated, "Amen."

Sliding back to her chair, Esther said, "Well, now we'll just wait and see what God's hand is gonna do. In the meantime, we keep on prayin', keep on watchin' and keep on sleepin' well. We'll just keep on keepin' on. Since God's gonna be takin' care of business there's no point in us worrying about it. So, what'd ya say you guys relax and watch some T.V? Remember our motto of how we are blessed?"

Scotty spoke first, "Too blessed…"

Before another word came out the other two joined him, "…To be stressed. 'Cause we're blessed by the best. Why should we worry about all the rest?"

Esther clasped her hands and held them under her chin. Tears found their way to the edge of her eyes, and she smiled. "That's right. Why should we worry about all the rest?"

Waynie spoke up immediately, "To the couch! Everybody to the couch! Gonna watch T.V. on the couch!"

The three others were already on their way to claim their seats.

Esther gave a big smile and nodded her head, "My boys."

Later that night Esther wandered down the hall to check on the boys. Both Waynie and Robert were asleep on their beds with their headsets on. She put her hand over her mouth and fought to keep the tears from coming. "Music, a sure remedy for a troubled heart."

She moved a few steps further and opened Scotty and J.T.'s door. Scotty was asleep on his side facing her and holding an unlit flashlight. J.T. was lying awake on his back. He tilted his head toward Esther and nodded with a slight smile. Esther blew him a kiss and smiled while closing the door.

In the hallway she gave a deep sigh and whispered, "Lord, I know you love dem boys, but we sure do need your help."

-11-
A DAY AT THE POOL

The June sun seemed to come early that day and gave promise that the day would be a warm one. The boys were looking forward to their Saturday trip to the community pool and did nothing to hide their excitement.

Robert, speaking with a Spanish accent asked, "Mommasita! When are we leaving for de poolo?"

Esther gave a little chuckle, "In a little while. Remember you asked me that already. I mean already-o."

Imitating a voice he heard on television he retorted, "So sorry my dear!"

"In a little while. In a little while. Goin' to the pool in a little while," chimed Waynie.

J.T. clapped his hands three times and went up on his toes signifying his approval and excitement.

To occupy their time before they were to leave for the pool the young men helped Esther straighten up the house.

Scotty collected the trash from all the rooms and brought it to the curb. Waynie vacuumed the living room rug. J.T. and Robert swept off the steps and the front and side porch. Soon it would be time to head into town and the pool.

The time of *soon* finally came. Esther rounded up the guys, "Okay, gentlemen. It's time to load up the van and head out." The young men scrambled to their rooms and returned just moments later dressed in their bathing suits and T-shirts with their towels on their shoulders. The previous year the boys had picked out the swimwear of their choice. They were each of modest length and seemed to match their personalities. J.T.'s was of a light blue color while Waynie's was bright orange. Scotty's bore several footballs, while Robert's was covered with pictures of various poses made by Shrek.

While Esther enjoyed being *at* the water, she didn't enjoy being *in* the water so there was no need for her to have a bathing suit. She simply donned a pair of long shorts and a tee shirt bearing the words, "Too blessed to be stressed."

Esther already had a large basket filled with their lunch waiting by the door. "Robert, be a darling and carry the basket for Ms. Esther, will you?" Robert didn't answer but scooped up the basket by the handle as he slipped out the front door. In short order the gang was loaded in the van and Ms. Esther was pointing them all toward a day of fun in the water.

They pulled into a moderately full parking lot and the team emerged energetically with each man carrying his towel around his neck and an orange life jacket draped over his forearm. They all wore tee shirts and flip flops. Esther leaned against the side of the van and called out, "Alright, sunscreen time! Come over here." The men gathered around her. "Now we need to be safe, and sunscreen will protect us from getting burned by the sun."

Esther, with her beach bag draped over her forearm, turned toward Waynie. Demonstrating with her hands, she said, "Waynie, put your hands together like this and I'll spray some sun screen on your hands." Then holding up the can she added, "This stuff smells a little like soap or lotion."

Waynie stepped forward and followed Esther's lead. She sprayed some on his hands and said, "Now wipe that on your forehead and face and the back of your neck." Waynie again followed her instructions and said, "Gotta be safe! Gotta be safe! No burns today!"

Then Esther asked, "How does it smell?"

"Smells good," Waynie answered. "Smells like soap. Smells like good soap."

"Good. Now put your hands out again." And again, Waynie did as he was instructed. Esther sprayed some more on his hands. "Now wipe that on both sides of your legs. Make sure you do front and back of both legs." Waynie did as he was told.

Esther said, "Very good. You did a really good job!" Then turning to the others, she said, "Now fellas, let me do the same for you. Put your hands together like Waynie did." Each of the boys held their hands together with their arms extended. Esther sprayed each set of hands. "Alright, now wipe your face and the back of your neck with it." Each man did what he was told sharing their thoughts on how it smelled. They repeated the procedure covering both of their legs.

Among the *extras* that Esther brought was a t-shirt for each of the guys. They felt more comfortable swimming with their shirts on so there was no need in protecting their backs from the sun.

When the gang was all sprayed down, Esther said, "I've got our passes. You fellas wait for me at the check in gate."

Scotty ran ahead without waiting for the others, while the other three men bounced along with Waynie and Robert chatting loudly.

Waynie exclaimed, "Gonna hit the diving board. It's at the deep end. Cannon ball time. It's groovy cannon ball time!"

Robert was still carrying their lunch basket and was swinging it back and forth while J.T. walked with Esther behind the group. She was carrying a towel for the lounge chair and a small umbrella for additional shade. J.T. carried the bag of extra clothing and Esther's lounge chair.

Robert remarked, "Cannon balls sink. You better know how to swim."

"I can swim," Waynie vented a bit defensively. "You know I can swim. I can swim a little."

"I can swim a lot. I swim like a champ!"

Waynie laughed and bumped Robert's shoulder with his own, "You swim like a chimp. Like a chimp is how you swim."

Scotty stood waiting at the check-in station. The rest of the gang joined him, and Esther moved to the front of the group and extended the passes toward the man at the gate. "Good mornin', Greg," she said smiling.

Greg smiled back, "Good morning Ms. Esther! Good morning boys!"

"Mornin' Greg," the boys called out with Waynie adding, "Cannon ball time!"

Greg gave a chuckle and said, "Yup, cannon ball time!"

Greg was engaged to Annie and was very familiar with the young men. He had been to their house several times with Annie and the two of them had grown close to the group. Along with teaching at the school, Greg managed the town pool during the summer. The pool was also open on weekends before school got out and after the weather warmed up. Today was the third weekend the pool had been opened and the crowd was beginning to grow. Several times, Greg had the young men over at the gym on a Sunday afternoon. He labeled it "Crazy Game Day." He emptied the storage room of just about every sports item. Basketballs, kick balls, volleyballs, wiffle balls, corn hole, and the badminton set were all put out for the pleasure of the guys.

One day he even brought out the archery equipment and taught the boys how to shoot. This made Annie nervous but ushered in quite a conversation at the dinner table that night with each of the boys telling Esther what great archers they were.

At the gate Greg waved each pass over the reader saying, "Welcome fellas! Gonna be a great day at the pool. Be safe and have a great time!" As each man moved through the gate, they gave Greg a high five. Robert was in front of Waynie. He wore three medals around his neck and had five ribbons pinned to his shirt. Greg gave him a quizzical look and waved him in. He turned to Waynie as if to ask, "What's up with that?" Waynie shrugged his shoulders, tilted his head to the side, and in a matter-of-fact way said, "Michael Phelps."

Greg understood completely and waved Waynie in saying, "I'll bet your cannon ball is going to empty the pool." Waynie nodded, "Yup! Big cannon ball time."

Moments later everyone had their life preservers fastened and had deposited their essentials at the base of Ms. Esther's lounge chair. Next came the whooping as they made their way to the pool. Waynie was out front and had made a beeline for the diving board with Robert right behind. T.J. and Scotty headed for the steps.

Waynie stood on the diving board as if to get the nod from the judges. He extended his arms over his head and ran off the board making a cannon ball the best he could. When he bobbed to the top, he asked Robert, "Good one hunh?" Robert simply affirmed, "Yup as he raced off the board himself.

The entire afternoon was filled with water and fun. They played tag in the shallow end, raced from one end to the other, and sat on the edge enjoying the warmth of the sun.

Meanwhile, Greg was having a somewhat heated conversation with Mrs. Edwards. She was a long-time member, and somehow equated the length of her membership with the weight of her opinion. Nodding toward two of the boys who were seated part way down the steps she groused, "I just don't think it's a good idea that's all. What if one of them gets hurt? Or what if they hurt someone else. More than one person has told me that they make them feel uncomfortable. All I'm suggesting is that we have a special time for them to swim. They could have the entire pool to themselves."

Greg crossed his arms and asked, "And when would that be? Sunday morning at five AM? Listen Mrs. Edwards, I know that you don't feel comfortable around those young men, but if you got to know them you might change your mind. Besides, they have just as much right to be here as anybody. They bought a membership just like everybody else."

Mrs. Edwards shook her head and gave a small sigh. "Well, be that as it may, I just don't think that everyone feels comfortable having them here." Turning toward Waynie standing on the diving board she added, "Now do you really think he should be in the deep end? What's he doing on the diving board anyway?"

Waynie bounced twice and hit the water.

When she turned back to Greg he simply stated, "I'd say a cannon ball. Look, I've been managing this pool for three years, and as long as the town hires me to run this place, the boys will be welcome here. I suggest you do your best to get used to that. Greg nodded his head to punctuate his sentence and walked away. Mrs. Edwards frowned and shook her head.

Greg walked to the edge of the pool where Waynie was climbing up the ladder.

Brushing the water off his face, Waynie asked, "Hey Greg! Did you see my cannon ball? How was that one? I do good cannon balls don't I Greg?"

"Yeah, I saw it. I'd say you scored at least an eight, maybe an eight point five. Not enough splash."

While climbing, Waynie said, "I'm gonna do another one. You watch, okay? Big cannon ball comin' up. Great big one comin' up!"

"Go for it big man!"

Robert turned from the snack bar with an ice cream cone in each hand. He took a few steps and came upon a five-year-old girl staring down at a lump of ice cream that used to be in her care. She alternated stares between the cone she was holding and the sweetness laying on the concrete. And then the tears began to come. Her mother knelt beside her and tried to console her, but her sadness was beyond comfort.

Without hesitation Robert said, "It's okay! I drop my ice cream too sometimes!" Extending one of the cones toward her and pulling one towards himself he said, "This one's J.T.'s. I can't give you his, but you can have mine."

With the back of her hand, the little one wiped her tears and took the cone from him.

The mother stood and said, "That's awfully nice of you! Thank you!" Then patting her daughter on the back, she said, "Katie, say thank you to the nice man." "Thank you!" she said while smiling at him and wiping her tears between licks.

From her lounge chair, Esther was able to witness the entire scene. Smiling she nodded and whispered, "A fine young man!"

As he approached J.T. at the table, he turned away from him, licked the cone twice and gave it to him after turning the cone's disrupted pattern away from him. J.T. received the cone without noticing the violation and bounced with joy.

-12-
SPECIAL CELEBRATIONS

Esther saw to it that noted holidays were special for the Bradford Street gang. When the day drew near, she decorated the house appropriately to surprise the young men when they arrived from work. Their families were always invited to dinner, and they all attended. Greg and Annie were welcome as well, but most holidays they spent with their respective families.

For Thanksgiving Esther put up posters of pilgrims and turkeys. The space on the table was almost completely taken up by *The Horn of Plenty* and an emphasis was placed on the blessings they had all received.

The parents brought various desserts and coupled with the meal Esther cooked made it a feast. Before eating, Esther asked each of the boys if they would share something they were thankful for.

Waynie spoke first. "I'm thankful for this food. Great food. We're having great food tonight."

Robert spoke next. "I'm thankful for Ms. Esther. She always takes care of us."

Esther nodded and fought a tear.

Scotty added, "I'm thankful for our parents." Everyone thought there would be a qualifying phrase but Scotty simply shrugged his shoulders signifying that he was finished.

The group turned their attention to J.T. He looked around the table, turned his palm up, and motioned with his hand that he was thankful for all of them.

Esther smiled broadly noting, "Each of us have been so blessed by God. We've got health, strength, friendship, and love. These are things that money can't buy, and people can't steal. We have so much to be thankful for!"

The entire table smiled and nodded in agreement followed by Waynie and Scotty clapping their hands.

J.T.'s father Alex asked the blessing, and the group enjoyed a great meal interlaced with a rich time of fellowship.

When Christmas approached, a small tree stood in the corner of the living room covered in lights with a basket of ornaments for the boys to finish decorating. Candy canes, stockings, and a manger scene were scattered throughout the living room.

Esther bought a birthday cake decorated with the words, *Happy Birthday Jesus.* After dinner that night, the entire group sang *Happy Birthday* to Jesus and enjoyed their special dessert.

When Easter arrived, palm branches, crosses, and a scene of the empty tomb were placed about the living room. Upon entering their rooms, the young men found a bag of various types of candy on their pillows.

Scotty offered Waynie a trade. "I'll give you my marshmallow chicken for your lollipop."

"Okay," Waynie answered tossing it to him. "I still have two from work."

J.T. held up his hand holding several jellybeans. He pointed at Robert's chocolate bunny signifying his desire for a trade.

"No way," Robert answered. "Chocolate's my favorite. "But you can have my marshmallow bunny."

J.T. looked down in thought. Then he raised his head, grinned, and poured the jellybeans on Robert's bed. Robert tossed the bunny his way and the deal was complete.

With each holiday, Esther was sure to carefully explain the meaning behind the celebration. Questions flowed like raindrops and Esther patiently and simply answered each one.

Each of the families arrived with gifts and food. The evenings were always rich with joy and love and everyone enjoyed the holiday festivities.

-13-
TROUBLE NEXT DOOR

One night, the gang was finishing up dinner when Esther asked, "Now gentlemen, how about some dessert?" The three boys cheered and J.T. pumped his fist and rocked showing his approval.

"But first, you gotta, *follow the beat.*"

Waynie repeated, "Follow the beat. We gotta follow the beat."

"We're good at this Ms. Esther," Robert chimed in, and J.T. nodded a second.

"Everybody got their hands in the ready position?" Esther asked.

"Yes!" the boys each responded as they moved their plates toward the center of the table and placed the palms of their hands on the table.

Esther announced, "Here we go!" Then with the palms of her hands she rapped out a simple beat and the boys repeated it. She followed this with another beat a bit longer and more complex, and the young men mimicked it as well. They continued with this exercise several more times with the men following it flawlessly. Then Esther clapped her hands several times signifying the exercise was over and announced, "Excellent! That deserves dessert!"

With that she exited to the kitchen returning in short order with a tray holding five bowls of ice cream. While the group enjoyed their treat, the doorbell rang.

"Who rang that bell?" Robert asked in a voice he learned from *The Wizard of Oz*.

"I'll get it" Esther stated as she pressed herself away from the table.

Esther Opened the door to find their neighbor standing there. Mr. Nelson was an elderly man who lived alone having lost his wife to cancer six years ago. He had been a man of average disposition but that left him when death took his wife. He seemed to be in a poor mood most of the time and had little patience for anything or anybody that disrupted his life. For the most part he kept to himself and stayed busy looking after the house, and his small dog. His entertainment came in the form of reading and watching television.

"Hello Mr. Nelson. Do you want to come in?" Esther asked.

"No thank you. I just came over to let you know that I don't appreciate the boys cutting across my yard on their way home. I spent all day Saturday raking and planting grass seed and they cut right across all of it and left big footprints in the mud."

Esther showed no alarm. She said, "I'm sorry Mr. Nelson, but are you sure it was my guys?"

"Who else could it be? They're the only…They left at least two sets of footprints across my yard and they tracked mud across my driveway. I don't expect them to clean it up, but I do want you to tell them to stay off my yard."

Esther began to get mildly defensive, "The boys know enough to stay off your yard…"

Mr. Nelson's emotions began to grow, "Those boys don't know enough of anything. They're mentally…challenged. They don't know enough to get out of their own way. When you all moved in here, I knew there would be trouble eventually."

Esther's emotions began to match the man's, "Mr. Nelson, if you'll wait just a minute, I think we can get to the bottom of this." Then stepping away from the open door she called the boys from the table, "Boys! Would you please put down your spoons and come here right now?"

The boys all gathered by Ms. Esther at the same time.

Looking at the group, she asked, "Boys, you all know Mr. Nelson, don't you?"

Sequentially the men all said, "Yup! Sure do! We do."

Esther's voice took on a gentle but firm tone. "Now men, I want you to tell me the truth. Did any of you cut across Mr. Nelson's lawn today on your way home from work?"

As usual, Waynie was the first to speak up. "No Ma'am! We never cut across people's property. It's not right. Not the right thing to do."

"We always stay on the sidewalk. It's safe on the sidewalk," Robert added.

Esther's voice began to gain its former firmness. Turning back to Mr. Nelson she said, "There, you see. The boys didn't do that. It must have been someone else."

Putting his hands on his hips, Mr. Nelson said, "Well the footprints were heading in this direction. If it wasn't them, then who was it."

Esther gave a heavy sigh, shook her head, and pursed her lips. Turning back to the boys she said firmly but gently, "Boys go into your rooms and bring out the shoes that you wore to work today. Don't stop to do anything else. Just bring them right here."

Without response, all three of the four young men walked swiftly to their rooms. J.T. just stepped aside and moved both hands away from his side showing that he couldn't do what was asked. Seeing this Esther asked, "J.T., where are your shoes?" Then the answer to her question came to her. "Oh, that's right. They're under the table. You took them off when we sat down to eat. I put them by the closet door."

Then pointing to the closet, "They're over there. Go pick them up sweetie and bring them over here."

J.T. stepped aside and returned in seconds holding his shoes.

Esther and the man stood silently facing one another. Esther broke the silence by saying, "The men only have one set of sneakers, and they wear the same ones every day."

Mr. Nelson simply nodded.

She took the shoes from J.T. and held them up as the men bounced back holding their own.

Esther pointed her thumb in the direction of the shoes and faced their guest. "Now, do any of these shoes look like they've been in the mud?"

Mr. Nelson glanced at the shoes and then looked down. "No. No, I guess not. I, ah, I guess I made a mistake. But I still don't want these boys on my property."

Turning to the young men she said "Okay guys. Go put your shoes back in your room and you can go back to your dessert."

The men scampered away while she turned back to Mr. Nelson. Using a firm but soft voice she said, "Mr. Nelson. I know your lawn is important to you. But understand this. These boys are a lot more important to me than grass seed and mud. In the future, I'll thank you to be sure of the facts before you go accusing them of something they didn't do."

The man looked down for a moment as if contemplating a reply. "I still don't want anybody on my property."

"I understand."

Then he turned and walked away. Esther shook her head as she watched him go down the steps.

-14-
THE TROUBLE KINDNESS BRINGS

The following Wednesday the boys were bouncing home from work. They were moving down the sidewalk two by two chatting as the walked. When they passed by Mr. Nelson's house Waynie noticed a wallet lying on the driveway by the driver's side of the car.

"Hey look!" A wallet! A wallet on the driveway," Waynie told the others.

"It's probably Mr. Nelson's. He probably dropped it," Robert said.

Scotty spoke up, "We can't go on his property. We can't go on nobody's property. Ms. Esther said so."

"But he may be looking for it and we know where it is," Waynie argued.

"Waynie," Scotty warned, "We can't go on his property. You're gonna get in trouble."

Robert agreed, "He doesn't like us Waynie. Let's go home!"

"Let's go get it and give it to him. Maybe then he'll like us," Waynie offered.

"No Waynie! Let's go home! We're always supposed to go straight home, Robert said.

Scotty added, "Yeah. Straight home Waynie. No stops."

Waynie turned toward the driveway and said over his shoulder, "I'm gonna give him his wallet. You guys wait here."

Robert called to him, "We're not waitin' Waynie. You're gonna get in trouble, but we're not waitin'."

Waynie walked a few steps and moments later he had the wallet in his hand and was walking toward the front door. He climbed the steps and stood before the door contemplating his next move. Waynie gave a heavy sigh and rang the doorbell. A few moments later Mr. Nelson opened the wooden door and then the storm door.

"What are you doing on my property? Stay off my property!" he bellowed.

Waynie was greatly startled and panicked. He let out a yell of fear, dropped the wallet and jumped off the porch skipping the steps.

Mr. Nelson said quietly, "I knew there'd be more trouble from that group."

He began to close the storm door when he looked down and spotted the wallet.

Waynie ran the rest of the way home without slowing down. He ran into the house and down the hall to his room. The other three boys had just come in and were in the kitchen talking to Esther. All eyes followed Waynie down the hall.

Robert told Esther, "Waynie's scared 'cause he went on Mr. Nelson's property."

"Oh Waynie! He knows better than that."

Robert continued, "he found Mr. Nelson's wallet by his car, and he was bringing it to him. Ms. Esther, we told him to come straight home-no stops-straight home. We heard Mr. Nelson yell at him."

"I see," she said. "Let me go and talk to Waynie. I'm sure he's upset."

Esther moved down the hall and knocked gently on Waynie's door. Waynie didn't respond so she opened the door and went in. Waynie was lying on the lower bunk and was facing the wall. Esther sat down on the edge of the bed. He turned and hugged her, wiping the tears from his face.

She held him for several seconds and Waynie leaned back and said, "I'm sorry Ms. Esther. I didn't mean to go on Mr. Nelson's property. I just wanted to give him his wallet. I thought it would make him happy and he would like us. I didn't mean to break the rules. I didn't mean it."

Esther struggled to keep from crying. "Oh, Waynie! You are such a special young man! Listen and try to understand what I'm going to tell you. I give you rules so that they'll protect you. You understand that don't you?"

"Yes Ma'am."

"But sometimes things happen, and it would be better to break the rules than to keep them. That's hard to understand so let me give you an example. Now pay close attention."

Esther paused and took a deep breath.

"Let's say you boys are walking home from the bus. Now you know you're supposed to stay on the sidewalk, don't you?"

Waynie nodded his head.

"Well, what do you think you should do if one of the other guys trips and falls into the street when a car is coming?"

"I should get him."

"Right! You should pull him to safety even though it means breaking the rules. See, sometimes the rule of caring gotta take the place of other rules. Do you understand?"

"I think so."

"Today, in Mr. Nelson's driveway, the rule of caring had to take the place of the..." Esther spoke in a deep voice, "*Stay off my property* rule. Does all this make sense?"

"Yes Ma'am. But he scared me when he yelled at me."

"I know. Sometimes when people don't understand things, they get angry. But I want you to understand that you really didn't do anything wrong and I'm proud of you for caring."

"Really? You're proud of me?"

"Sure honey! I wish more people had a heart of caring like you do. Now I'm going to call Mr. Nelson and explain the whole thing to him. When he finds out the truth, I'll bet he is thankful for you too."

"You think so?"

"There is no doubt in my mind."

Waynie was about to respond when they both heard the doorbell ring and one of the boys in the living room yelled, "Doorbell!"

Esther patted him on the back and said, "Let me get that. We can talk some more later If you want." She stood up and made her way down the hall to the front door.

When she left, Waynie reached over, turned on the music, pulled his headset on and put his feet on the bed above.

When Esther opened the door, she found Mr. Nelson standing there with his head slightly pointed down. In his hands were some home-made cinnamon cookies. Quietly he admitted, "It seems I've made a big mistake."

Esther tried not to give him a smug look and said, "Yes. I think so. Please come in."

The other three young men were watching television when Mr. Nelson stepped in. Robert nudged J.T. sitting on the couch beside him and all three turned toward him cautiously.

Esther said, "I'll go get Waynie."

Esther knocked on the bedroom door but got no response, so she entered. Waynie was laying on his back with his eyes closed and tapping the mattress with his hands. She tugged on the cord to the headset and immediately his eyes opened. He slid the headphones off and heard her say, "Waynie, you have a visitor in the living room."

Waynie put the headset on the pillow as he sat up. "Okay," he said, "Annie or Greg. Still a visitor."

Esther led him down the hall. When Waynie entered the edge of the kitchen his eyes caught sight of Mr. Nelson and he froze.

"Come over here darling," Esther said pulling him gently by the arm. "Mr. Nelson has something he wants to say to you."

Waynie walked slowly toward him. "No yelling. No yelling right?"

The three on the couch stood up to get a better view.

"No yelling" Mr. Nelson said. "I'm sorry that I yelled at you. I shouldn't have done that. I didn't understand that you were returning my wallet." He extended the plate of cookies toward him, "I'm sorry. Here are some cookies for you and the other guys."

Waynie stepped a little closer and took the plate while looking down. He was clearly intimidated.

Esther spoke up. "Waynie what do you have to say to Mr. Nelson?"

Still looking down, Waynie timidly murmured, "Thank you!"

After an awkward pause, Mr. Nelson said, "Well, I better be going. I'm sorry son. You folks have a good night."

Esther replied, "We will. Thank you."

Mr. Nelson exited. Esther closed the door and turned to face Waynie who was staring at the cookies.

"Well, Waynie, what do you think?"

"Mr. Nelson was nice. No yelling. No yelling at all."

"Yes. He finally realized you did a good thing."

"Yes. A good thing."

Esther took the plate and walked to the kitchen and placed it on the counter. "Now you and the guys can have one cookie each. I don't want you to spoil your dinner."

That announcement brought the other young men flocking to the kitchen for their share. A slight smile was found on Waynie's face as he took a bite.

-15-
PIZZA NIGHT

That Friday night brought Greg and Annie to the house. They carried a small tray loaded with different types of donuts. When they came in, they found Waynie and Scotty seated on the floor of the living room playing "Go Fish" J. T. and Robert each had a magazine and were sitting on the couch looking at the pictures.

The boys bounced up from their spots and raced to the door to meet their guests. Esther took the donuts from Greg and placed them on the counter. High fives and hugs were exchanged as the couple came into the living room and sat down.

After visiting for a few minutes Esther announced, "You two are right on time! Now listen everybody. In honor of our special guests tonight, we're gonna to have a 'make your own pizza' dinner. And then we'll have some donuts and draw to see what movie we'll watch."

"Gonna be a great night!" Waynie declared. "A really great night!"

Robert spoke up in the voice of Clint Eastwood, "Go ahead, make my day!"

Scotty spun on his heels sharing two quick dance moves he had seen on television.

"Alright," Esther said. "You boys go wash your hands and let's sit down.

Three of the boys scrambled down the hall while J.T. headed for the kitchen sink. When they returned Esther gave the instructions. "Okay. I've put out everything you need to make your pizza. Now boys, we're gonna let our guests go first. Greg and Annie, you guys get busy, and you boys help me set some things on the table."

Greg and Annie moved to the counter, while the young men gathered several items from the other side of the counter and began putting out the napkins, glasses, and pouring the sodas.

When Greg and Annie finished their preparation work, they moved to the table and the men moved to the other side of the counter where they joined Esther.

Under Esther's guidance, each boy worked his way around the counter passing various ingredients back and forth while working on his meal.

Robert covered his with tomatoes and peperoni. J.T.'s held a variety of meats while Waynie went the artistic route making a giant smiling face of Pepperoni. Scotty was very conservative in that his pizza only had an extra dose of sauce and the normal amount of cheese. Esther made her own with a mixture of cheese, mushrooms, and ground beef. She put all the pizzas on three different trays, set the oven temperature, and joined the others in the living room.

When the entire group was together, Greg announced that the guys had to play a game called "Living Room Survival." He glanced at Esther and received her nod of approval. Then as he took the lamp off the end table and moved the chair by the desk to make it more accessible, he explained to the boys that the living room was not a normal room.

"The couch is an old tree log. The carpet is acid and quicksand, and the only places you can touch are the chair, the end table, the desk, and the couch. You gotta find a way all the way around the room without getting burned by the acid or drowning in the quicksand." All the boys nodded indicating their understanding.

"All right," he said. You guys get on the tree log." With excitement the young men lined up on the couch. "I'll be the referee and Ms. Esther and Annie will be the cheerleaders."

The men scrambled on the couch each vying to go first. Robert led the way followed by Waynie and J.T. Scotty brought up the rear. With only a few close calls, they all made it around the room and returned to the top of the couch, standing and laughing in victory.

But Scotty was in the back and in the excitement of completing the task, was bumped, and tripped off the end of the couch. One of his feet hit the floor. He popped it right back up but not without the other guys noticing.

Robert and Waynie turned and pointed at Scotty. "You're dead! You fell in and you're dead!" J.T. pointed at Scotty and jumped up and down pumping both fists.

Scotty defended himself. "No, I'm not dead! I have special metal clothes on, and I can't die."

"Yes you did die. I saw you fall in the acid and quicksand, and you died, Robert called out.

"No I didn't," Scotty argued.

Esther grabbed the remote and pointed it at the boys while smiling at Annie. She pressed the remote several times and said, "This thing's not workin'. Must be the batteries." Both ladies chuckled.

Things started getting somewhat heated, so Greg jumped in. "Hold it guys! I'm the referee. I saw what happened." He stepped into the center of the room and imitating an NFL official he touched his hip to turn on his microphone and said, "After viewing the play, the player had finished the course and landed in fair territory on the log. Mission accomplished!"

Scotty cheered "Yes!" and pumped the fist of his right hand toward his hip. The other men nodded but kept silent.

Then Esther announced, "It's time for us to draw to see what movie we're gonna watch tonight. She picked up a small note pad and tore off six pieces of paper. Then she reached into the drawer and pulled out several pencils. Handing a slip to each person she continued, "Now everyone put their first initial on the paper and fold it in half." When they completed the task, she extended a bowl to them and said, "Now put your paper in this bowl." When they put their papers in, she mixed them up.

Esther remembered that Scotty hadn't won their drawings in quite some time, so with the others looking on, she discreetly spotted his name, slid his paper to the side, and pressed it against the edge. Then she raised the bowl over her head and continued to *mix* the papers up. She pulled one slip out and announced Scotty as the winner.

Scotty raised both clinched fists over his head and yelled, "Yes!" and immediately walked over to the television and opened the cabinet holding all the DVD's. He knelt on the floor and pulled several choices out looking at their pictures. The other boys joined him to see what movie they would be watching that night.

In a few moments, Scotty stood up and held up his choice for everyone to see. Robert announced, "Indiana Jones!" We're gonna watch Indiana Jones."

"This is a good one! One of my favorites," Waynie declared. "Dr. Jones is my hero!"

"Mine too!" Robert agreed.

Scotty exclaimed, "Mine too. I think he's everybody's hero."

J.T. shook his fist in the air and nodded his head several times.

"I wish I could be him, "Waynie announced. "He always gets the money and the girl. Gotta have both. Gotta have both, the money and the girl."

Scotty retorted, "I just want the money."

"Okay everybody," Esther explained. "Let's go over to the piano. J.T., I believe you have a song inside you that you can play for us." J.T. nodded and the gang moved toward the piano.

J.T. slid onto the bench and Greg said, "I didn't know he could play." "I didn't know either," Annie added. Waynie, Robert, and Scotty leaned on the back side of the piano while Esther pulled up chairs for the couple. She stood to the side of J.T. smiling.

J.T. started playing a weak version of "Chopsticks." He finished and Greg and Annie applauded. J.T. smiled and nodded, but it was more of a prank move than that of appreciation.

Esther smiled as well, but not the smile of approval. She and the men were in on the joke. Annie and Greg seemed to clue in that there was more to the story and gave each other a confused look.

Esther looked at J.T. and said, "Now J.T., do you think there's a little more inside you that you can share with us?" J.T. smiled and nodded toward a pair of sunglasses sitting on the far end of the piano. Scotty grabbed them and handed them to the performer. J.T. put them on and smiled. Then he began rocking back and forth in Stevie Wonder style.

He placed his hands on the keyboard and opened with the Johann Sebastian Bach's composition Fugue #2. Annie and Greg were captivated. Then for the next five minutes his fingers flew up and down the keyboard making music that left the couple slack jawed and speechless. Next, J.T. transitioned to Neil Diamond's "Sweet Caroline" and the entire group joined in with a loud "Bah, Bah, Bah" at the appropriate places.

When he finished everyone applauded except Greg. He just stared froze by what he had just witnessed.

Speaking above the noise from the gang, Esther turned from the open oven and announced, "Pizza's done everyone. Have a seat at the table and I'll bring it to you. Now remember, it's hot so be careful."

"Hot pizza" Waynie exclaimed smiling. "Gotta have hot groovy pizza."

Robert spoke up in his John Wayne voice, "Yup. Gotta have hot pizza pilgrim!"

Annie and Greg just smiled and shook their heads.

When everyone was served Esther asked Greg to say the blessing. Greg nodded and everyone bowed their heads and folded their hands.

"Dear Lord, thank you for this day, for these guys, for Ms. Esther, for Annie, and for pizza. Amen."

The group offered a unanimous, "Amen" and they all enjoyed their version of pizza followed by a showing of "Indiana Jones."

-16-
TRINITY COMMUNITY CHURCH

The following Sunday found the boys with Ms. Esther at Trinity Community Church. The church was only about two miles from their home and Esther made sure they all were dressed appropriately and on time. When they arrived, they found their usual seats about midway towards the front. They had been coming to Trinity since they moved into the house and felt at home immediately. The church was a non-denominational one and was a mixture of black and white races.

Pastor Corby was a middle-aged black man who was well liked by both the members as well as the community. He held Esther's young men in high regard and always made it a point to speak to each of them. The boys felt at home in the church and were readily accepted and looked after by the congregants. To the delight of the boys, Greg and Annie attended the same church. They normally sat a few rows behind the guys on the opposite side. This meant that Esther had to often pat the leg of one of the guys who couldn't resist the temptation to turn part way around and wave at their two friends. Invariably, at some point in the service, all four of them had turned around and gained a return smile and wave from Greg and Annie.

At the start of the service, the minister of music stood up. Mr. Tony Dobner was a heavy-set white man in his thirties and was gifted in playing both the piano and the guitar. He had a strong well-trained voice and often sang solos to the delight of all those present. The people liked him and appreciated him, and his feelings toward them was mutual. He nodded his head toward the piano player and announced, "Good morning, everyone! It is so good to see you here on the Lord's Day. Please turn to hymn number thirty-seven in your hymnal and let's stand and sing together."

As the introductory music started, Waynie leaned over to Esther and informed her, "This is my favorite song. I love this song. It's my favorite."

Esther whispered to him, "Well then, why don't you let the Lord know by singing it out."

When the music called for the people to join in singing, Waynie lifted his voice and sang loudly. He was not gifted with a good singing voice but made no attempt to sing more quietly. With a smile on his face, and joy in his heart he belted out part of the first verse and the chorus of the song that he had grown to love. Being that he didn't know any more of the hymn, he swayed through the rest. This brought several smiles from those around and an oversized grin from Esther.

Later in the service the choir sang softly while the offering plate was passed around. Each of the boys participated, bringing smiles to the faces of those close by as well as Ms. Esther.

Scotty passed the plate to Robert and whispered rather loudly, "No free rides! Nobody rides for free." Those close enough to hear it did their best to conceal their laughter.

After some special music, the Pastor preached an energetic and inspiring sermon on treating others the way you want to be treated. The *Amens* were audible evidence that the congregation was connecting with his words. At the conclusion of the service Pastor Corby stood outside the building and greeted everyone as they departed.

He greeted Esther warmly and shook hands with each of the boys. When he got to Robert, he was greeted by the voice of Barney Fife.

"Great sermon Pastor! Great sermon! You just can't hear enough about sin these days."

Pastor Corby was clearly puzzled. "Yes. Yes, you're right," he muttered as Robert moved on.

Waynie was next. He saw the confused look on the Pastor's face and held his palms up and away from his side. He shrugged his shoulders and simply said, "Barney Fife." Then he joined the others and headed to the parking lot.

The pastor raised his eyebrows and nodded giving a look of understanding to no one in particular.

-17-
CELEBRATION?

Friday was a special day. Not only because it meant no work on Saturday, but because it was the third of July and it ushered in the July fourth celebration in town the next evening. As the weekly calendar moved, the excitement of the upcoming adventure had grown. And the entire trip down the sidewalk to work brought comments about the upcoming outing into town to watch the fireworks.

"I hope we can see all the fireworks tomorrow night!" Waynie bellowed. "I hope we can see 'em all."

"Yeah," Scotty affirmed. "I hope there's lots of 'em."

"Ms. Esther said it will be a great show," Robert told the group. "She said she talked to somebody who goes every year and it's a great show."

"Gonna be a great show! A really great show," Waynie proclaimed. "Lots of rockets and stuff. "A great big show."

J.T. skipped a few steps and put both hands in the air as if imitating an explosion.

"Early dinner first and then we go downtown," Waynie told the group. Ms. Esther told me that."

Soon, the boys were in sight of the bus line and picked up their pace. "Annie! Annie!" they called out as they got close to the bus stop. Scotty began running and the other three followed suit. Annie was midway up the line holding her morning coffee.

"Annie, fireworks tomorrow night!" Scotty yelled.

"Yup. Fireworks on Saturday night guys," she told them. "Greg and I will meet you in the parking lot. We'll save a spot for you, and we'll all enjoy the show."

"Yeah! Gonna enjoy the show! Really big show," Robert agreed, sharing a poor imitation of Ed Sullivan.

For J.T. and Scotty, this would be their first experience in watching a live fireworks show. They all had seen displays on television and Waynie and Robert had been there in person, but this first for the other two brought anticipation and excitement to a new level.

On Saturday, after dinner, Esther instructed the men to each get a lawn chair from the storage room and put them in the van. They scrambled to comply and had the van loaded in short order. Esther came out with a basket of snacks and small flashlights and asked Scotty to carry the canvas bag holding their waters. She knew it would be a late night and made sure she was prepared.

As the sun had become just a speck on the horizon, Esther and the gang wheeled into town and searched for a parking place in the large lot of the abandoned Sears building. They unloaded the van and began looking for Annie and Greg while carrying their chairs and helping Esther with the bags. The parking lot was full of cars. Scattered groups of people were sitting in chairs, on blankets, and in the beds of trucks.

The temptation to run hit strong in each of the boys prompting Esther to order, "Stay close fellas! We'll find 'em, but we gotta stick together. Nobody runs. You guys got me?"

"We gotcha," Robert spoke for the group.

Esther struggled to keep up as the pace of the boys grew. A couple of times she had to remind them of her previous instruction. They walked quickly toward the front of the store knowing that their friends had made plans to arrive a good bit earlier than them.

Moments later, J.T. jumped in the air a couple of times and pointed. He had spotted Greg and Annie. The others called out, "Greg and Annie! Greg and Annie! We found 'em Ms. Esther! We found Greg and Annie."

The couple was sitting in chairs with a blanket in front of them and a cooler between them. When they heard the boys, they both stood and turned around.

"Hey fellas!" Greg hollered.

Annie followed with, "Hi guys!"

"We found you! We looked for you and we found you! Waynie called out. "Gonna be a great night! Fireworks and friends. A great night!"

"You bet! Greg agreed.

"Fireworks into space!" Scotty proclaimed. "I'll bet they go a mile high!"

"Maybe higher," Greg offered. "Just hope they don't punch a hole in sky and let all the air out."

This comment greatly puzzled the boys and Robert and Scotty looked at each other with a mixture of concern and confusion.

"He's only kidding guys," Annie explained shaking her head. "You know you can't take him seriously."

"I knew he was kidding," Waynie was quick to say. "You can't put a hole in the sky. Greg was just kidding."

Moments later, their camp was set up. Their chairs were arranged in a semi-circle with each facing the park where the fireworks would be launched shortly after dark. Though their eyes drifted about them, the focus of the men kept coming back to the area where the rockets would explode. They were getting anxious and impatient and kept asking anyone who would listen how much longer before the explosions would start.

And when darkness had sufficiently settled in, the rockets took off. The gang joined the gathered crowd in their *ooohs* and *aaahs* as one blast followed another. J.T. pointed upward and pounded his chest and moments later Scotty responded, "I feel it too. It's splodin' in my chest."

"That's the sound wave hittin' ya," Greg explained "Pretty cool hunh?"

"Yeah, really cool," Robert agreed.

As each successive explosion took place lighting up the night sky, the boys commented on which ones were their favorite. After a while Annie noted that new favorites or multiple favorites were happening all the time. This made Greg, Annie, and Esther smile while joining the boys in naming their own favorites.

Though the display lasted about thirty minutes, it seemed to go on endlessly. Greg mentioned the *Grand Finale*, to the young men which would signal the end of the display and punctuated it with "Wait 'til you see that. It's unbelievable."

This brought questions about whether or not the last explosion was it. Greg assured them, "Fellas, when it comes, you'll know it for sure."

And moments later it did come! Spying the trailing flames of twenty or so rockets, Greg announced, "Guys, I think this is it."

"This is it! This is it! This is it!" the boys repeated.

And what a display it was! It seemed like there would be no end to the blasts and fiery flames. The entire sky was lit up as if it was day-light. The *ooohs* and *aaahs* from the parking lot population were louder and more pronounced than ever.

And then the air was filled with complete silence. Nothing was left except the smoke trails of the multitude of rockets that were launched. Then without prompting, the entire crowd burst into loud applause. Taking their cue, the boys clapped and cheered as well.

"Well, that's it for another year," Esther announced. "Let's get our stuff together and find our van."

The group began to gather things together when several loud pops from firecrackers were heard right behind them. There was just a hairsbreadth of a pause and the rest of the pack exploded. J.T. rushed to Esther's side in obvious fright. Without hesitation Scotty jumped to Esther's other side. The two boys clung to her with their faces displaying their fear. J.T. pumped his legs in place and moved his head back and forth.

Esther's immediate reaction was to pull the boys close. Greg's im-mediate reaction was to attack the fools who would dare to scare his friends. He turned and took a step in the direction of two grown men bent over laughing. This sight enraged him all the more. But before he could take his second step, Annie grabbed his arm.

"Babe wait! It's not what you think!" Then pointing to the side of the car she said, "Look at her."

It was then that Greg noticed the red-faced woman standing behind the men. He also noticed a chair laying on its' side and quickly un-derstood what had happened. The men thought it would be funny to light a pack of firecrackers under the woman's chair. The prank was never meant to scare the boys. He took a deep breath and mut-tered, "Idiots." Then he turned to check on the two boys.

They were still clinging to Esther. He went over to them and put his hand on each of their shoulders. "It's okay guys. Just some knuckle-heads having fun. That wasn't meant to scare ya."

Greg's comment was followed by a man's voice behind them. Everyone turned in his direction and found the two men standing there. "Hey guys, we're sorry. We didn't mean to scare ya. We were just trying to scare Emma." The other man joined in. "Yeah, we weren't trying to scare you guys. Sorry about that."

Greg was about to both accept their apology as well as share some of his own thoughts when he was preempted by Waynie.

"You shouldn't scare people. It's not nice. It's not nice to scare people. You scared my friends."

"I know," One of the men receded. "We're sorry. We won't do that again."

With that, they turned and walked away.

J.T. and Scotty loosened their grip on Esther's waist and took a couple of deep breaths. Soon the pack was carrying their cargo and heading through the parking lot toward their vehicles.

"Not such a good idea after all," Esther thought. "Maybe not such a good idea."

-18-
ROMANCE IN THE AIR

On Sunday night Greg and Annie were on a date at Lorenzo's Italian Restaurant. It was an upscale place and at the top of their favorite places to eat. The atmosphere was filled with romance with candles centered on each lace covered table. There was an area that served as an unofficial dance floor which remained mostly empty. Soft music was constantly playing, and the staff were gifted in their timely attention to each table. And Lorenzo's food was magnificent. The chef who prepared it was gifted and had won three local awards over the last five years. The level of the food, service, and atmosphere were met by the level of the price of the meal. So, it was understandable that Greg and Annie weren't found there often. But occasionally, they would splurge and treat themselves to a special night out. And being that this was the second anniversary of their dating relationship, tonight was one of those special occasions.

Greg and Annie had met two years earlier at the courthouse. Annie was doing an internship while attending law school. Her area of concentration was in estate settlements, but the internship at the courthouse was a paid one and between paying for her undergraduate degree as well as law school, she was carrying a sizable amount of debt. She worked for the magistrate checking people in who were assigned jury duty. And one of those people was Greg. Annie caught his eye immediately and they both engaged in small talk while she took care of registering him.

"Good morning," she began. "And your name is…"

"Greg," he answered. "Greg Novak."

Thumbing through her cards she asked, "With a *C*?"

Smiling, Greg answered, "No, with an *N*."

She grinned slightly, raised her head from the cards and explained, "I meant your first name."

"I know. I was just kidding. Greg with a *G*."

"Got it. And your last name is Novak?"

"Yup, Novak."

"That's an unusual name. Where does it come from?"

"Well, my great-grandfather was from Czechoslovakia. It means Novice." Smiling, he said, "I guess I'm not supposed to be an expert at anything.

Annie smiled and tipped her head to the side commenting, "Wow! That's an interesting perspective."

"So, what's your name?" he asked.

"Annie. Annie Foster. It's English and I think it means, the lady is in charge here."

Greg joined her in a little chuckle. She handed him his pass and name tag. He wheeled around and headed toward the courtroom.

The case Greg was assigned seemed to be a moderately simple one. A man had been accused of robbing several houses in the area. He had teamed up with a woman (not his wife) and she dropped him off at the houses she had cased. The man cleaned out the house of anything of value then called for her to return and pick him up.

When he was arrested and they searched his house, several guns were discovered. This complicated things in that it was now a federal offense. It took three days for the trial to be completed. Normally this would have frustrated Greg, but he saw it as a way to *run into* Annie.

The hardest part of the case was determining which houses the man was responsible for robbing. After two days of discussion, the jury decided that the man was guilty of robbing seven houses, and due to a flight threat, he was kept in custody without bail. Sentencing was set for next month. During her trial, the woman was later found guilty of assisting in the robberies but was released on bail.

On the third day, after leaving the courtroom, Greg went out to his car to find a parking ticket on his windshield. The members of the jury had been told where to park and were given assurance that if any of them received a ticket, they could bring it back and it would be taken care of by the court.

Greg conveniently saw it as the movement of the hand of God, giving him another chance to talk to Annie. In a bold move he asked her out for coffee. Thus began their dating relationship. Less than a year later, the two became engaged.

At Lorenzo's they each enjoyed their favorite meal with Greg ordering Lasagna while Annie had veal parmesan. Conversation was light with each sharing main points of the past week. Then came dessert. Both Greg and Annie had a sweet tooth and never passed up a chance to fill it with a treat. They decided to share the *Volcano cake* and when it arrived, it didn't disappoint.

While slowly devouring their dessert, Greg told Annie, "I think I'll take the boys to the gym next Sunday and let them mess around for a while."

"Sounds great," Annie concurred as she reached out and held both his hands. After a short pause she said, "Can I ask you a question?"

"What if I said no?"

"I'd ask you anyway."

Greg smiled.

"You do such a great job with those boys. They really like you and ask about you almost every time I see them at the bus stop."

"Well, I enjoy being around them too. Now, is there a question connected to this or did I mishear you?"

Annie tipped her head to one side explaining, "Well I was wondering, if I weren't in the picture would you still spend so much time with those guys?"

Greg smiled. "Maybe. I don't know. But if you're asking me if I'm being nice to them just to get to you, you're wrong."

Annie moved her head to the other side. "Oh really!"

"Yeah. Really."

Greg took a deep breath and looked down trying to gather his thoughts. "Yeah. Really" He repeated. "Let me tell you something I haven't told anybody in a very long time." Greg leaned to the side and pulled out his wallet. Reaching in, he pulled out a picture and handed it to Annie.

"See this little boy? That's Kevin. He was my cousin. He was a couple of years younger than me. When we were growing up, he lived across the street from us and we kinda grew up together."

Annie looked at the picture and nodded.

"He had Down Syndrome." We always got along great and spent a lot of time together. He died before I got out of college 'cause he also had a heart condition. They were surprised that he lived as long as he did."

Taking his hand again, Annie sympathized, "I'm so sorry!"

"Thanks. Kevin was eighteen when he died, but his mind was only about seven. One day, when I was in seventh grade, we went down to the malt shop. It was our favorite place to go hang out. Our plans were to get a milk shake and then hit the movies. When we were on the sidewalk in front of the store, I saw a girl from my class inside named Mary Alice. To my junior high mind, she was the most beautiful girl on the planet."

Annie grinned taking in every word.

"She looked out the window and smiled at me and my mind was gone. I left Kevin outside and went in to talk to her. I swear I only talked to her for a few minutes, but when I looked out the window, Kevin was gone."

Annie shook her head gently, "That's so scary."

"Oh, yeah. I ran out the door and jumped down the steps. I looked as far as I could in each direction but didn't see him. Luckily, I went to my left and about 50 feet away was an alley. And there was Kevin surrounded by three kids that I didn't know. They were high school guys, and they were slapping and pushing Kevin around."

Annie's eyes were locked on Greg's.

"I ran down the alley and yelled as I went. When I got close enough, I could see Kevin's face. He was scared to death. I didn't stop to ask what was going on, I just ran to the closest guy and pushed him over some trash bags. One of the other guys grabbed me and knocked me down. I got a couple of punches to the face and then they ran away."

"That's terrible!" Annie exclaimed. "There's never an end to mean people!"

"Well, Kevin helped me up. He said a quiet, 'Thank you' and told me I was a hero. I got a bloody nose, and a split lip. But I gotta tell ya somethin'."

"What?"

"I was only twelve, but as best as I can remember, I never felt so much like a man in my life. And every time I see or listen to one of those boys, I see my cousin Kevin."

Annie stood up and leaned over the table toward Greg. "And now, you're not just a man, you're my man." Then she planted a kiss on his lips.

When she sat back down, Greg looked her in the eyes and in a serios tone said, "Do you know what my parents taught me without saying a word?"

"What?"

"I'll never forget this. They taught me that people are to be valued not because of what they do, but just because they're people."

Annie smiled and laid both her hands on his, "Can I tell you something?"

"Sure."

"You're a really special guy!"

Greg looked down for a moment. Then looking up at her he asked, "Can I tell you something?"

"Yup."

Then standing up and leaning over the table he quipped, "You have great taste in men!" Then he planted a quick kiss on her lips.

Annie giggled, "Yeah I know!"

Annie turned her head as if to tune into the music. *One in a Million You* by Larry Graham was playing.

"Oh, I love this song," Annie said as she stood up. "Let's dance!"

Looking at the dance floor Greg resisted, "No one's dancing."

Without hesitation, she grabbed his hand giving it a tug. "We are!" The rest of the world faded away while they were in a world of their own.

-19-
HOMECOMING AT TRINITY

The following Sunday was a special one at Trinity Community Church. It was *Homecoming*. The church had been founded nineteen years earlier by Pastor Henry Russell. He was a good man from Atlanta and was well-received in the community. During his tenure, the church grew to a steady number of about seventy-five people. James served there for nearly twelve years until he retired, then James Corby took over.

The church could normally seat about 150 comfortably. But with it being homecoming and so many people being invited from the past and present, it was more than full. Chairs were placed in the aisle and along the back wall and the choir was instructed to remain in the choir loft. Esther and the boys sat in their normal spot and didn't seem to be bothered by the tight seating arrangement.

At the start of the service, all the guests were welcomed by Pastor Corby, special music was played, and a short time of welcome and fellowship followed.

As part of the service Tony Dobner had written a special song about their church. Not only was Tony a very capable worship leader but he was also gifted in writing music and lyrics. Before coming to Trinity, he had written three songs that were bought and sung by two different bands in Nashville. Two of the songs were welcomed by the public with a fair amount of success, but the third one did very well reaching the top twenty for two weeks on the charts.

Tony had also written a few ditties for some local companies and four of them were bought and used widely by two of them. Tony and April Jenson performed the duet which was enjoyed by the congregation the chorus of which came to be a theme song for the church.

"Cause Trinity is blessed,
Yes, Trinity is blessed,
Oh, Trinity is blessed!
By the good hand of the Lord."

Following the song, Pastor Corby gave an energetic and inspiring message about the purpose of God's church. Those present were moved by it and a general sense of a renewal of commitment was felt throughout the congregation.

After James closed the message in prayer, Howard Graham, the chairman of the deacons rose to make a special announcement. Joining James at the podium, He remarked, "My friends, you know how blessed we are. The good hand of the Lord has truly blessed us here at Trinity."

This comment was followed by several *Amens*.

"One of the greatest blessings the Lord has given us is found in our pastor and friend, James Corby. It's no secret that James and Viola love the Lord and they love us." Again, more *Amens* were shouted.

Howard looked at the couple and motioned for Viola to join her husband at the podium. He continued, "Many of you may not be aware that the Corby's will be celebrating their thirty-first wedding anniversary next month." This brought enthusiastic applause from the crowd. "The church body has gotten together to give a gift to our friends." Those gathered sat in rapt attention and all eyes were glued to their pastor and his wife.

"We've made arrangements for Pastor Corby and Viola to spend three days at Virginia Beach. Their hotel and all their meals will be covered. We just want them to go in freedom and have a fantastic time relaxing, celebrating, and enjoying themselves."

The congregation rose to their feet in applause as Howard slid next to the couple and presented them with an envelope holding the gift. James and his wife grinned widely as they accepted the gift. After an extended time of cheers Pastor Corby spoke to the church body.

"My friends, you know how much Viola and I love you and the ministry the Lord has called us to at Trinity. Ministry always carries a lot of weight with it, but we are blessed that so many of you have joined us in carrying the weight the Lord has placed in our hands. Thank you so much, and God bless you!"

The congregation remained standing and erupted in applause again. James waved to the crowd and pointed toward Tony Dobner, who moved to the center of the platform. As James and his wife stepped off the platform Tony said, "Friends, let's close in prayer and make our way to the fellowship hall so we can enjoy a great meal the ladies have prepared for us." He closed in a short prayer and the church made its' way over to have lunch together.

Almost everyone present in the church worked their way to the fellowship hall. Inside the building was a long table filled with food On the opposite wall was another long table with desserts of every kind, iced tea, and bottles of water. Jerry Meyer, one of the deacons grabbed a microphone and called for everyone's attention.

"People, if I can get your attention for just a second. I'd like to ask the Lord's blessing."

The room quieted down completely and those who had already started eating put their forks down. Everyone bowed their heads.

"Dear Lord, we thank you for once again providing a great meal for us. Please bless the food to our bodies and this fellowship to our spirits. In the name of Christ we pray, amen."

The room followed with an "Amen," and the noise of conversations picked up immediately.

Esther and her young men worked their way along the tables and found a place to settle down to eat. They were joined at their table by Greg and Annie.

"Good food. Good food," Waynie declared pointing at his plate full of food. "Always good food at the church."

Scotty rocked back and forth and added, "Dessert comes next. I know what I'm gonna have."

J.T. nodded excitedly while pointing at Scotty.

"I'm so excited for James and Viola. I hope they have a great time at the beach," Esther shared.

"I'm sure they will," Annie added. "They sure do deserve it. Whose idea was it anyway?"

Greg said, "I think that came from the deacons. They're always on top of things."

When they finished their meal, they made their way to the dessert table and the boys brought back plates loaded with a helping of almost every dessert on the table.

They all were enjoying their dessert when Tony Dobner's voice was heard over the speakers. The room grew quiet as he said, "Hey friends. I hope you're enjoying your lunch." Nods of affirmation followed.

"We've got plenty of food and dessert so help yourselves to seconds if you want. If you go home hungry, well, that's your own fault."

Chuckles of laughter were heard throughout the room.

Then he grew serious, "As you're enjoying your meal, I want you to know that our music team has been working on a special project in the area of musical encouragement.

The title *musical encouragement* was not a foreign term to the church. Several times over the last few years it had been used to describe a song that had been prepared and targeted toward one of the members.

When Martha Abernathy turned 100, the team showed up at the nursing home and sang to her. Martha had been an active member of Trinity for several years before her family could no long take care of her. She had been in the care facility for four years when she achieved the aging milestone. She still had control of most of her faculties, but her body was beginning its rapid decline.

The music team had arranged for her to be ushered into the dining area where several family members and a host of residents had gathered. When she came in, the group cheered, and she was wheeled to a table holding a large cake with 100 candles on it. Martha kept looking around at the group as her face glowed.

After singing *Happy Birthday* to her, the music team broke out in song. It was a special song that held memories of Martha growing up in Hanson County. Her skills both as a dancer and a seamstress were mentioned as was her love for her husband and children. Her strong faith in the Lord and a special place in heaven were part of the chorus. Her tears readily streamed her face and her smile never dimmed.

While eating cake she thanked everyone for being there and made an inadvertent comment that brought laughter to the room. She said, "This is wonderful! Thank you! Thank you all for being here! I will never forget you if I live to be 100." The chuckles in the room helped her realize what she said, and she followed it with, "Oh, yeah. I already did that. Well, I guess it's true." And again, laughter filled the room.

On another occasion the church had four students graduating from high school and one graduating from college. The church held a luncheon in their honor and the music team had come up with a song dedicated to them.

The song was up tempo and talked about studying, overcoming, lack of sleep, extra credit, and success.

The chorus was,
"Late nights, early days.
Fighting through the knowledge haze.
Workin' hard, takin' tests,
Writin' papers, doin' your best.

It was not expected as part of the days' celebration, but the musical team had prepared a special song for Esther and her boys. Tony announced, "Today we want to encourage a special group who is part of our church."

As Tony began speaking, two women and one man got up from their seats and joined him at the front of the room. "They're here every Sunday and they always want to be involved in everything we do. So, this song of encouragement goes to Esther and the boys."

All eyes turned to the table where Esther and her gang were seated. Esther wore a smile of surprise and Waynie told the others, "It's a song for us. They're gonna sing a song for us!" The others smiled broadly and J.T. rocked in his chair and pumped both fists in the air.

Then Tony turned and nodded to the man at the sound table and the up-tempo music began. After a few introductory notes the group sang:

"No pushing aside,
No whispers about.
No pointing with noses,
No pity and doubt.

We don't keep our distance,
We don't leave them out.

They're part of our family,
We won't turn them out.

'Cause there's still room,
Yes, there's still room.
They'll aways be room, (in our world….)
For guys like them.

There's still room,
Yes, there's still room.
They'll aways be room, (in our world….)
For guys like them.

They work in the shop,
They work day by day.
And just like the rest,
They earn their pay.

They're happy to come,
And worship the King.
They make us all happy,
As we hear them sing.

There's still room,
Yes, there's still room.
They'll aways be room, (in our world….)
For guys like them.

There's still room,
Yes, there's still room.
They'll aways be room, (in our world….)
For guys like them.

Ms. Esther sure does love them,
And gives them such great care.
She enters into their world,
And lives with them there.

And they love Ms. Esther,

'Cause she's their house mom,
And with her whole heart,
The house is a home.

Soooo...."

And as the team began the final chorus, the rest of those gathered joined them.

"There's still room,
Yes, there's still room.
They'll aways be room, (in our world....)
For guys like them.

Ooooooh, there's still room,
Yes, there's still room.
They'll aways be room, (in our world....)
For guys like them."

And with the final note, the room erupted in applause. Then the table where the gang was seated became crowded as the people swarmed to their sides. High fives, fist bumps, and hugs came in abundance. It was a historical homecoming for Trinity Community Church.

After lunch Esther and the young men headed home smiling and talking the entire way.

Waynie pronounced, "A good day. A good day at church. We had a really good day at church."

Scotty talked about the food saying, "I got plenty of food. Dessert too!"

J.T. pumped his fist in the air several times.

Robert declared, "We got a song. We have our own song. They sang a song to us." And with that he led the crew in a partial rendition of their song. They didn't have the verses down but decided on their own version of part of the chorus.

Robert began with, "Still room for us guys, yes there's still room for us guys." The others joined in repeating the few words they held onto for several repetitions.

Esther continued to smile noting that her heart was as full as it had ever been.

-20-
PARENTAL BLESSINGS

On Wednesday evening, Scotty's parents came to the house bringing several bags of groceries. It was not unusual for the boys' parents to drop in from time to time. Esther and the gang were always glad to see them regardless of whose parents they were, and they welcomed them with open arms. Pete and Adele were very familiar with Esther and were immensely grateful for the care she showed all the young men.

After putting the groceries away, Esther checked on the meal in the oven while the others settled down in the living room. The conversation meandered from work to health, to Scotty's sisters. One of boys brought up the topic of the group's song. Pete and Adele requested a rendition, and the boys were more than happy to comply.

Waynie nodded his head as he began and the other two joined in before he finished the second word, "Still room for us guys, yes there's still room for us guys, there's still room for us guys."

Pete and Adele smiled and clapped their hands. And with a broad smile, Esther shared with them about the homecoming celebration at church.

"I can't tell you how thankful we are that you guys go to a church that would do something like that," Pete remarked.

Shaking her head, Adele added, "That is really a special group of people you guys are involved in."

"They sure are," Esther noted. They welcomed us in from the day we first showed up."

Waynie explained, "We're family. When we go to church we go to our other family."

Hearing the bell from the oven, Esther announced that dinner was ready. The boys and their guest popped up and headed for the dinner table. Adele helped Esther take the food from the kitchen while Scotty poured the milk.

The group enjoyed a large meal of salad, bread, and lasagna. The meal was topped off with Scotty's favorite, cherry pie.

When it was time for Scotty's parents to head home they thanked Esther and gave hugs to all the boys. Scotty walked them out to the car, hugged them again and watched them pull out of the driveway. When their car was out of sight, he spun about and bounded up the stairs.

While Esther was in the process of cleaning up the dinner dishes, she came across an envelope with her name on it. It was obviously left by Pete and Adele. She opened it and found a twenty-dollar bill with a note that simply said, "Thank you for all you do! Coffee money."

She leaned against the counter, shook her head, gave a heavy sigh, and smiled. "Another blessing!"

-21-
BACK YARD FUN

On Saturday, late in the morning, Annie and Greg arrived bringing hot dogs, ice cream, and soft drinks. The plan was for them to spend the day with Esther and the young men. They would play games and then cook out on a grill that Greg had bought off the internet and gave to the house.

They entered the house without knocking and Greg announced, "Hey guys! We're here!" Esther was in her bedroom getting ready for the day. J.T. and Robert were watching T.V. and Waynie and Scotty were in Waynie's room looking at magazines and listening to music. Those in the living room got up and came to the couple. Because of the music, Waynie and Scotty didn't hear them come in. But Scotty happened to glance out the window and notice Greg's car. Moments later the two were standing in front of Greg and Annie as well.

Waynie said, "Hey you two! Good morning!" Both Annie and Greg put an arm around each of the boys' shoulders and gave them a squeeze. Before the hugs were over, Esther was in the living room getting hugs of her own. She grabbed the ice cream and put it in the freezer. "I made some fresh iced tea. Do you two want some? I also have coffee."

"I'll have a cup of coffee," Annie answered.

Stepping toward the kitchen Greg announced, "Coffee sounds good."

Esther grabbed a couple of mugs off the drying rack and poured each of them a cup. She knew that Greg liked his black and Annie always added a couple of spoons of sugar. She poured herself a cup and the three of them sat at the table while the boys went back to their previous activities.

"How're the wedding plans coming?" Esther asked. "Everything lining up?"

"Yeah!" Annie declared. "We've got most of the big stuff done. Now it's just the little details we have to decide."

"Like how you're gonna give me everything I want and obey me all the time," Greg challenged while grasping Annie's hand.

Annie took her other hand and patted the back of his. "And how you're gonna stop living in a make-believe world."

Greg shook his head gently, looked at Esther and remarked, "And now the struggle begins."

Smiling, Esther took a sip of her coffee and proclaimed, "Buckle up! It's always a roller coaster!"

Greg nodded. "Just three more weeks and the ride officially begins."

Annie turned to her and asked, "You guys got your invitations, didn't you?"

"Sure did! A couple of weeks ago," Esther said smiling. "When I showed the guys the invitation, they all jumped up and down cheering. I think they may be more excited that you are. They're each taking turns moving it to a different place in the kitchen." Pointing to the kitchen she said, "Right now, it's on the side of the fridge. Waynie wanted to keep it in his room, but he was vetoed by the others.

"Doesn't take much to get them going does it?" Greg asked.

"No, it sure doesn't," Esther replied. "I wish more people could get excited like them. I think the world would be a happier place."

"Yeah, I know what you mean" Annie agreed. "I remember how excited they were when I showed them my ring. You would think they won the lottery."

Nodding his head, Greg said. "And remember last year when we watched the Super Bowl together? I thought they were gonna break the couch. J.T. was so excited I thought he was gonna speak for the first time."

"I don't think there's anything that can bring him his voice," Esther explained with a slight grin. "But he has his ways of letting us know what he wants."

"And you have a way of reading each of those guys," Annie suggested while pointing at Esther's heart.

Esther turned her head toward the living room. "Well, we have kindred hearts."

Standing up and taking a gulp of his coffee, Greg stated, "Hey, I left the charcoal in the car. Let me go get it." He abandoned his mug on the counter and headed for the door.

Turning to the living room Esther called out, "Hey Robert, why don't you help Greg get the charcoal out of the car?"

Robert got up and began walking toward the door, keeping his eyes on the T.V. Then he turned to Greg and in his Elmer Fudd, voice announced, "Let's go you silly Wabbit."

Greg smiled. "Yeah, let's go Elmer."

The two men left the house and brought the charcoal and the lighter fluid to the grill in the back yard. Greg opened the bag instructing

Robert to hold the lid open. The lid could stay up by itself, but Greg knew that it was important to make Robert (and the other three) feel needed. He poured most of the bag in the grill and told Robert to close it. They would add the fluid when it came time to start grilling. In the meantime, he and Robert would return to the car and bring a couple of games out.

When they got to the car J.T. was standing there. It was obvious that he wanted to help as well. Greg pulled out several things that he had picked up from the school including a kick ball, soccer ball, a couple of Frisbees, and a corn hole game. Greg carried one of the corn hole boards while J.T. and Robert carried the other. They returned to the car and picked up the rest of the items and before long, had everything set up in the yard and were kicking the soccer ball around.

In no time Waynie and Scotty had joined them, while Esther and Annie stood at the window finishing their coffee and enjoying the show. Waynie made himself the goal by spreading his legs. A near miss by Robert to the apex of his legs convinced Waynie to turn around. This position, though less painful, was quickly abandoned as well.

A few minutes later the boys were joining Greg in tossing the frisbee. A throw may have gone fairly well but it was usually followed by a non-catch. Soon Greg convinced the boys to play *Target disc.* He would call out an object and the boys would make a throw at whatever he named. The garbage can, maple tree, fence post, and downspout were targets and the young men did surprisingly well. After each connection with the target the group would celebrate. Soon chants of "We're number one," and "Score, score, score," were shouted by the group.

Moments later, Annie and Esther came out to join the group. Esther carried a tray of hot dogs, while Annie carted the basket of *fixins'.* She placed the basket on the nearby bench and opened the grill lid.

Seeing the tray Waynie shouted, "Hot dog time!"

"Not yet," Esther remarked. "I think we should cook them first. What do you think Anne?"

Showing a face of disgust Annie affirmed, "Yeah. Nothin' worse than a raw hot dog."

Greg was moving the corn hole boards into place while Annie poured lighter fluid on the charcoal. The coals were lit and within moments the flame was dancing and begging to heat up their meal.

The men had played the game in the gym before but never caught on to the scoring. Yet they understood that the goal was to get the bean bag in the hole. They started by throwing overhand, but with some coaching from Greg learned to toss it underhand. Anytime a bean bag landed on the board the entire group celebrated. Winning and losing never entered the picture but boredom did and after several tosses each interest in the game waned and it was deserted.

Greg knew the young men loved playing *hide and seek.* He had plans to include that in his list of games while they waited on the grill to do its job. It was immediately suggested by Scotty that Greg be *It* so he moved over to the edge of the house to hide his eyes and count to twenty.

As soon as he made his move toward the house, the boys scrambled to find places to hide. The rules were, they had to stay outside and in the back yard. Esther and Annie laughed as they watched each of the guys move from place to place trying to decide where to hide. Greg counted slowly as he peeked and saw each of the men struggling to settle on their spot.

As they ran from place to place, Robert was loudly singing Bruce Springsteen's song *Born to Run.* The other two joined him and sang their modification of the song with words each of them was somewhat sure about, "Cats like us, baby we were born to run!" Even after they found a hiding place they continued to sing quietly. This brought a chuckle to Greg and the ladies.

When Greg finally reached the number twenty, he shouted, "Ready or not, here I come!" Immediately he spotted both Robert and Scotty squatting down behind the dead maple tree. He pretended not to notice but before long came across the boys. By touching each of them he put them in *Jail* on the back steps.

As he was escorting them to confinement, Robert said to Scotty, "Told ya. You picked a bad place. That was a bad place to hide."

Immediately, Greg jumped in. "No, it was a great place to hide. It's just that I'm a champion hide and seeker."

"You are?" Scotty asked.

"Yup. In fact, I won a gold medal at the hide 'n seek Olympics."

He completely ignored Annie's *Don't tell them that* look and continued.

"Ya know, there's even some talk that I'm gonna be in the hide 'n seek hall of fame."

"Really?" Robert asked. "Like in baseball?"

"Yup! Just like baseball. Not only that, but after me and Annie get married, I'm going to China to compete in the hide 'n seek world championships."

Annie cleared her throat, "Now it's getting a little too deep. Make sure you clean your golden shovel big guy!"

Greg just smiled and nodded her way.

After putting both boys in *jail*, Greg turned to locate the other two. He took one stride away and noticed J.T.'s foot sticking out from under the wooden steps. He immediately yelled and went after him making sure not to move too fast so J.T. could make a run for it. He chased the young man to the corner of the lot and had him trapped. When he tagged him, J.T. put his head back and completed the motion of someone laughing hard.

J.T. was put in *Jail* with the others. Now to find Waynie. As soon as he stepped away from the others they burst out in song, "Cats like us, baby we were born to run. Cats like us, baby we were born to run."

Scanning the yard Greg couldn't get an eye on Waynie. Then he found the clue he was looking for. The plastic garbage bag was sitting behind the trash can. As he approached the garbage can he said loudly, "Now where could Waynie be? He's got to be hiding around here somewhere."

Then standing next to the can, he quietly grabbed the handle on the lid. With a quick pull, he yelled, "Ahaa!" and yanked it off exposing the back of Waynie's head. Waynie stood up quickly and tried to escape. But the edge of the can proved to be too high for him and he fell over backwards bringing the can with him.

A loud pop was heard as Waynie's head hit the ground. He lay there motionless with his eyes closed. Greg was sure the young man was hurt and was afraid that the injury was serious.

Kneeling and shaking Waynie's shoulder he asked, "Waynie, Waynie! Are you okay?"

In seconds, Esther and Annie were standing next to him. The other boys stood behind the ladies and peered around them to get a view of their friend.

Greg tapped Waynie's shoulder again, "Hey buddy, are you okay?"

Waynie opened his eyes and gently rolled over to his belly without making a sound.

"Waynie, are you okay?" Greg asked again.

Then Waynie slowly pulled his knees beneath him and gingerly stood to his feet. He looked at the silent group before him. Then in an instant, he made a funny face and dashed away while singing, "Baby we were born to run!"

The laughter that came from the group drained the energy from Greg and he didn't bother to chase him. Waynie was named the winner and the episode became a topic of discussion for months to come.

-22-
WEDDING JOY

Three weeks later and Greg and Annie were wed at Trinity Community Church. The ceremony was a simple one, with Pastor Corby officiating. Greg's dad had passed away six years previously, but his mom, brother and several relatives were able to attend. His brother stood beside him as his best man and two men he worked with at the school served as groomsmen.

Annie came from a large family and had quite a few family members in attendance. Her mom was seated in the front row while her dad walked her down the aisle and joined her mother after the giving of the bride. Annie's two sisters and two brothers were there as well as several cousins, aunts, uncles, and her eighty-two-year-old grandmother. Her older sister Melissa served as her Maid of Honor and her other sister Madison and a friend from work rounded out the bridesmaids.

After comments from the pastor, a song, the vows, the exchange of rings and several Bible verses, Greg and Annie were pronounced husband and wife. A closing prayer of blessing was given, and the newlyweds made their way down the aisle.

As they passed the row where Esther and the boys were seated, Waynie could not help himself and gave a thumbs up while calling out, "Way to go Annie! Good job Greg!" Those within hearing distance, smiled and nodded.

Scotty stated, "Nice wedding guys! Nice wedding!"

Robert pulled out his Porky Pig voice mimicking, "That, that, that's all folks" and the boys joined him in laughter.

Because the fellowship hall at the church was being renovated, Greg and Annie had rented out the Lions Club social hall. It had ample space for the 175 guests and was located just a few blocks from the church. The hall was well decorated by Annie's sisters and a few friends. Each table was garnered with a beautiful white tablecloth, a mixture of flowers, gold chargers, white plates, a set of silverware, light blue colored napkins, and a red candle. Esther and the boys were seated toward the front on the left side of the room with three of Annie's co-workers. In no time at all the boys were engaged in conversation with each of them.

The bridal party was introduced and seated at a long nicely decorated table at the far end of the room. When the couple of the evening was introduced, the entire room stood to their feet applauding and cheering. At the appropriate time, the DJ dismissed each table to make their way to the food bar. The catered meal was complete with sliced ham, chicken, green beans, mashed potatoes, a roll, and a cupcake for dessert. The drink table held water, lemonade (Annie's favorite), and iced tea. Servers were stationed at each area to help the guests work their way along the line.

When Esther and the boy's table was called, Esther instructed the men to let the other three go first and then she said, "Now boys, don't make any comments about the food. Just take whatever they put on your plate and say thank you. Do you understand?"

Each of the boys either nodded or verbally consented. With that, they joined the rest of the crowd in getting their serving. While in line, Scotty removed his toothpick and took a sip of one of the glasses of lemonade. He made a face, looked quickly around, and slid it back on the table without notice. Waynie caught the eye of one of the servers and couldn't resist a comment. "Good food! Good food at a groovy wedding. Gotta have both, A groovy wedding and good food." Each of the boys got what they wanted and sat down to enjoy their choices.

After a short time Annie and Greg were called to the dance floor for the bride and groom dance. They held each other tight as the song, "Loving you" by Elvis played to the delight of the crowd. Scotty got up on cue and shook his legs in response. At the conclusion of the song Robert stood, swung his arm and said loudly and predictably, "Thank you! Thank you very much!" Several seated at the nearby tables joined in applause bringing a smile to Robert's face followed by a short bow.

After the couple's dance Annie and her father hit the floor and moved to the tune of *Butterfly Kisses*. This brought tears to both dancers as well as a majority of those watching. Then the rest of the crowd was invited to the dance floor and began to gather.

When the newlyweds sat down Waynie quickly came over. Turning to Greg and following Esther's direction, he asked, "Hey Greg, can I dance with Annie?"

"Sure Waynie. But be careful. I just got her you know."

Ignoring the humor Waynie said, "I'll be careful. You know I'll be careful. I'm always careful."

They entered the dancefloor as Earth, Wind, and Fire belted out "September." Annie moved easily to the music, but Waynie, not so much. His moves were mostly stuttered but that didn't seem to bother him or Annie. While still moving, Waynie shouted to her, "Annie, you look good. You look really good. You are really happy too, aren't you?"

"Waynie, I've never been so happy in all my life."

"Then I'm happy too. I'm really happy for you! I really am. Greg's a good man. He's really a good man. A really good man."

She gave him a hug. "Thank you Waynie. I think so too!"

When the song was over, Annie turned to find Scotty ready to join her in another dance. This didn't seem to bother Waynie, and he took his seat. Next, Annie danced with both J.T. and Robert at the same time.

As was always the case, the boys had a great time with Annie and the crowd seemed deeply appreciative of her kindness.

After several more songs, Esther's voice was heard over the crowd. Holding the microphone in one hand while holding up her other one for attention she announced, "Ladies and gentlemen, may I have your attention please? My guys and I are so happy and excited for Greg and Annie. So as a special gift to the bride and groom, the young men have prepared something they wanted to share with the couple of the hour. I present to you, the Bradford Street bucket band boys."

Without knowing what to expect the crowd broke into enthusiastic applause.

Then all their attention went to the table where the boys were seated. Robert had his tie fastened around his forehead and his sleeves rolled up, while the other men had only removed their jackets. On the floor in front of each of them was an empty five-gallon bucket turned upside down.

With the palms of their hands, J.T. and Scotty began banging out a simple beat of seven hits. Robert and Waynie followed by repeating the beat. Then Robert and Waynie rapped out a beat a bit longer and the other two followed. This went on for four more series of beats and then all four men joined together in a complicated beat. The tempo increased for over thirty seconds and ended with Robert hitting the side of his bucket and sending it into a chair five feet away.

The crowd erupted in applause, whistles, and shouts of praise. All four young men stood up and held their buckets by the handles while bowing several times. Esther's smile communicated the pride she carried for her guys.

A short time later the departure of Greg and Annie arrived. A car waited next to the entrance. The crowd gathered outside the hall armed with bird seed and bubbles. Esther's boys stood closest to the car and when they had emptied their hands of bird seed, joined the crowd with cheers. Greg's handshake for each of the boys was followed by a hug from Annie.

Waynie patted Greg on the shoulder warning, "You take good care of our Annie Greg!"

"You know I will."

Robert spoke up in his Clint Eastwood voice, "We know where you live punk!"

Greg laughed. "Got it Clint. We'll see you guys next week when we get back."

Scotty teased, "Will you do any fishin' or will you be too busy kissin'?"

The boys all laughed.

Greg joined in their laughter, "Mostly kissin.'"

In a unified voice the young men groaned, "Ohhhh Greg!"

Waynie punctuated the comments with, "Fishin' and kissin.' Yup. Lots of fishin' and kissin.'"

Esther raised her hand and said, "Alright. You boys stop that now. It's time for them to go. Now you two have yourselves a safe trip and we'll see you when you get back."

"We sure will!" Annie and Greg said together.

They drove away amid more cheers from the crowd and Waynie and Robert making kissing sounds and laughing.

-23-
JUDGMENT

On Tuesday night the gang was gathered around the dinner table. Esther had cooked their favorite, chicken-pot pie. The young men enjoyed it then put their dishes in the sink. Finishing that, they all sat back down and prepared their taste buds for dessert.

"Dessert time," Esther announced. "Tonight's payment is a song, a joke, or a rhythm."

Robert raised his hand. "I've got a song!"

Then Scotty spoke up, "And I've got a joke!"

"Well," Esther remarked, looks like tonight we'll have a double payment. Scotty, you go first."

Scotty cleared his throat and wiggled with excitement in his seat. "What's green and red and goes round, round, round?" After a short pause he said, "A frog in a blender!"

Esther looked down and shook her head.

"You didn't let us guess. We didn't guess," Waynie protested.

"I know. 'Cause you don't know it," Scotty countered.

"That's daskustin' anyway," Robert groused.

"Yeah, that's gross!" Waynie added.

"Alright you guys," Esther admonished. "Robert, give us your song."

Robert pulled his chair closer to the table and reached into his pocket. He pulled out a pair of sunglasses and slid them on. Then in a Johnny Cash type voice, he sang, "I fell into a burning ring of fire. I went down, down, down, and the flames went higher..." He then faded realizing he didn't know the rest of the lyrics.

Scotty got excited. "That's John Wayne. He's doing John Wayne! I like that song!"

"It's not John Wayne dummy head!" Robert countered. "It's Johnny Cash. Johnny Cash sings that song."

"Yeah, Johnny Cash," Scotty realized. "That's who I meant. I get them mixed up. And I'm not a dummy head. I just got mixed up. You get mixed up too sometimes."

Esther jumped in. "Calm down gentlemen. You know how I feel about you callin' people names." She stood up and headed to the kitchen to retrieve the cookies they would be having for dessert.

J.T. clapped his hands and smiled at the sight of the plate of cookies. The other faces joined his and moments later the room was quiet except for the sounds of the men making noises of enjoyment.

"Now finish your dessert," Esther ordered. "Then get yourselves cleaned up. That means wash your face and hands and brush your teeth. We're going over to Dr. Spieglemeyer's office tonight for your checkup. He's nice enough to see all of you during his off hours and I don't want to keep him waiting."

As the young men finished the last bite of their cookies, Waynie blurted, "I'm Dr. Spieglemeyer, may I help you? I'm Dr. Speiglemeyer, may I help you?"

The table broke out in loud laughter. J.T. smiled, rocked back and forth, and pointed at Waynie.

"Okay guys. Go get ready," Esther repeated. "And remember to wash your face and hands and brush your teeth."

As the boys walked down the hall Scotty stated, "I wonder if nurse Carol is going to be there. She's ugggly!"

Waynie agreed, "Yeah, she's ugly, ugly, ugly."

The other two boys repeated, "Yeah, ugly, ugly, ugly."

Waynie said, "Turn your head and cough. Just turn, turn, turn, your head and cough!"

Robert protested, "No! I hate that. I don't like anybody down there! Maybe he won't have to do that."

The doctor's office was just a few miles away in the town of Brookvale, and it didn't take long before the group was climbing the steps to enter. Through a friend at church Esther had learned about the doctor and since their first appointment, they had been coming there for their medical needs.

Daniel Speiglemeyer had been practicing medicine for over twenty years. He was a middle-aged, moderately balding man, who carried a scar on his forehead that he received from an encounter with a drunk driver when he was in medical school.

He knew the scar would capture the boys' attention, so he filled them in on the details during their first visit. Surprisingly, the young men didn't ask any questions and never drew attention to it, much to the relief of Esther.

The check-ups were always quick but thorough and never carried a charge. The doctor counted it an honor to be able to do his part in helping Esther with the boys.

The boys' checkup went well. They all seemed to be in good health though Waynie and Robert were a bit overweight. And much to the boys' annoyance, they did have to turn their head and cough.

Nurse Carol was there, and the young men had a hard time keeping themselves from laughing. Carol was not unattractive. Her boyfriend Michael was clearly attracted to her. If anything, she was rather plain looking with her straight dark hair and her slightly round figure.

When the boys climbed into the car, Scotty softly chanted, "Ugly, ugly, ugly." This was followed by Robert repeating it, "Ugly, ugly, ugly." Next Waynie joined in repeating, "Ugly, ugly, ugly." Then all three boys chanted loudly, "UGLY, UGLY, UGLY."

Finally Esther ended the increasing noise by saying, "Enough! Be nice!" The car quieted down, but in the darkened car, the boys nodded at each other silently mouthing the words, "Ugly, ugly, ugly."

-24-
THE DARK DAY

When Friday came the young men were standing at the bus stop wearing their usual back packs and ball caps. They talked to a few of the others while waiting for their ride. They each made several comments about Annie not being there and how much they missed her.

The day at work was uneventful and over soon. They normally worked about six hours each day and headed home at the conclusion. They were excited about "No work tomorrow" and talked about it several times during the day.

Together, the young men walked down the sidewalk toward home. As usual, they slowed down as they approached a near by pond. The pond was on the edge of a person's property and wrapped around from the back of the house toward the road. It wasn't abnormally large but came within thirty feet of the sidewalk.

Many times, people could be seen nestled in chairs with a line and a pole. The young men never really took to the idea of fishing, so they never had cause to ask for permission. Their normal habit was to spy a small stone and toss it as far as they could into the pond while making a wish. And before they got within throwing distance, they each had found their prey.

Standing in front of the pond they took turns in no particular order, heaving their stones. J.T. went first. After looking down, as if in thought, he threw his underhand. It fell well short of the pond but bounced close to the edge.

"It still counts," Waynie said. "You can still get your wish."

Robert stepped forward and in his Jimmy Stewart voice from "It's a Wonderful Life" said, "I wish I had a million dollars." He sent his stone flying landing it about ten feet into the water. With the first ripple he yelled, "Hot dog!"

Waynie who was next pleaded, "I wish I had a giant chocolate chip cookie." In a late release, his stone hit the ground a few feet before the pond. "It still counts" he declared. Just like J.T's. It still counts."

Scotty was the last to throw. "I wish I could win in the Olympics," he announced as he took two steps forward and heaved his stone from the grass. The stone landed about three feet into the water, but the boys were focused on where he was standing. He was on someone's property, a clear violation of Ms. Esther's rules.

Pointing at him, Waynie shouted, "Ohhh! You're on their property. You're not supposed to be on someone's property."

Robert joined in, "You're in trouble Scotty. We're gonna tell Ms. Esther."

"No! don't tell her! I didn't mean to," he begged.

Right away, the threat disappeared. "We won't tell. We know it was an accident," Waynie said.

The boys made their way home and when they came within sight of the house Scotty began to run challenging, "I'll race you to the steps!"

Waynie declined, "Go ahead. I'm not racin' No racin' for me!"

"Me neither," Robert added. "Too hot."

"Too tired" Waynie groused.

Scotty never looked back but ran on ahead with his backpack bouncing back and forth against him while he held his cap in place. The other three just strolled along chatting about throwing rocks and making wishes.

Scotty mounted the steps and stood on the porch breathing heavily while waiting for the others. When the boys came to the edge of the property, he turned and went inside. "Ms. Esther! We're home!" he called out. Hearing no reply, he stepped toward the kitchen. Then he turned and saw her in the overstuffed chair in the living room. "Ms. Est…"

Even with an impaired mental capacity, Scotty understood that something was terribly wrong. He raced to her side and knelt beside her placing both hands on her forearm. She didn't move and Scotty somehow knew that the worst possible thing had happened.

From the porch the others heard Scotty cry out, "No Ms. Esther! No! Don't leave us! Don't go! We need you Ms. Esther. Ms. Esther, don't go!"

The young men raced inside. They found Scotty still kneeling on the floor with his forehead on Esther's arm and his face awash in tears.

Waynie and Robert jumped to their knees, "No Ms. Esther! No! No! No! We need you Ms. Esther! Please don't leave us. No!"

J.T. stood behind the three boys with his hands on Waynie's and Robert's shoulders. Then it happened. For the first time in their lives and possibly his life they heard the raspy voice of J.T. as he loudly hollered, "NOOOOOOOOOOOOOO!"

-25-
GRAVESIDE

The boys wore their suits and sat on the front row for the graveside service in the small cemetery behind Trinity Community Church. They had spent the last few nights in their own home with Greg and Annie serving as temporary guardians. The day Esther died, Greg had driven over to the Social Services office, filled out all the paperwork, and had it immediately approved. What would happen next was anyone's guess. But for the time being the guys would be looked after with the least amount of disruption from the life they had come to know.

The tears that Greg and Annie had shed for Esther were matched by the tears they shed for the boys. Each night they could hear the young men wailing on their beds in unfettered grief. They did their best to console them, yet their words of comfort were no match for the pain in their hearts.

A good-sized crowd was gathered at the cemetery. Esther had become a living example to them of love and sacrifice. The young men sat still staring at the casket. They were drained of their energy by their loss and confused about where life was taking them.

Pastor Corby was visibly upset during the eulogy. He had gotten close to Esther, and it was clear that he would miss her terribly. After a congregational song, a prayer, many positive memories of Esther, and several comments on Scripture readings, he closed the service with prayer.

The boys were led to the coffin where they were handed a flower from the ones perched on top. They each smelled the flower and hugged it with both hands. Then they each put their hands on the coffin and fought courageously to control their tears.

The crowd stood and passed by the casket with more tears being shed. Many of them paused beside the coffin, placed their hand on it, and offered up a silent prayer. Then those gathered walked together for a light lunch in the fellowship hall. Greg and Annie walked with the boys holding their arms around each of their shoulders.

Waynie asked Greg, "How long can you stay with us?"

"For a while. We have special permission to stay at your house."

Waynie smiled, "That's good! That's real good. You stay with us."

Scotty turned to Annie, "Can you make us breakfast every day? Ms. Esther always made us breakfast. Can you make us breakfast?"

"Of course!" Annie answered, pulling Scotty closer to her. "I can make pancakes and French toast, bacon, and eggs. Anything you want."

"Can you cut the crust off my toast?" Robert asked. Ms. Esther always..." Then the sadness of the moment cut off the rest of his sentence.

Greg pulled him closer and gently patted the back of his neck. "It's okay. You're gonna be okay."

Annie was quick to respond, "Yeah, I can cut the crust off your toast, and I'll even cut the toast off your crust."

Greg nodded at her comment and noticed the satisfied look on Robert's face.

In the fellowship hall there was a long table adorned with a white tablecloth and covered with all types of food. There was potato salad, corn, green beans, mixed salad, chicken, corn bread, ham, pineapple casserole, and a host of other choices. The end of the table held iced tea, water, juice, and coffee. A side table was placed on the nearby wall for all the desserts. Chocolate and vanilla cake, fruit cups, pudding, Jell-O, an assortment of cookies along with several other items guaranteed to satisfy any sweet tooth.

The young men were ushered to the front of the line. They made their way along commenting on the food as they went. Greg and Annie followed them closely being ready to help if needed. They soon found out that their help was not necessary as the boys seemed to do well enough on their own.

Picking up a drumstick Waynie commented, "I like chicken. Gotta have some chicken." Then he spotted the corn. "And corn! Corn is real good! Gotta have some of that too!"

"Potato salad," Robert stated. "That's my favorite."

Along with filling his plate with food, Scotty was filling his pockets with the tooth picks he was pulling from the bowl of fruit on the table. Annie saw what he was doing but said nothing.

J.T. just rocked back and forth nodding his head as he helped himself. He hadn't spoken again since the day of Esther's death.

When the four men got to the dessert table the unpredictable happened. Looking beyond the table, Waynie spotted a man named David. He had seen him several times in church over the last couple of years and had even spoken to him a few times. David was standing near the wall talking to another gentleman whom Waynie knew by face but not by name. David was a middle-aged white man with a short beard and a balding head. He wore a white shirt and a black and red striped tie that fell a few inches passed his buckle. What Waynie noted most was his waist size. David had the look of a man who hadn't missed a meal in his entire life. His belly hung down loosely making his belt buckle a stranger to daylight.

Waynie's eyes were locked on the man. Getting the attention of his three companions, he pointed at David. The others recognized him right away. Then Waynie reached down to the molded pile of Jell-O sitting on the tray before him. He shook the tray and the Jell-o quivered with the movement. As Waynie moved the Jell-O, he pointed at the belly of David. The other boys recognized the connection and burst out in such laughter that those in line leaned forward to get a glimpse of the cause of the commotion.

Annie didn't make the connection, but Greg knew exactly what was happening. He grinned at the humor but felt more satisfaction in the fact that the boys had found a distraction. He knew that humor had healing potential and thought that perhaps the healing had begun.

-26-
SITUATIONAL CONVERSATIONS

The next day, Greg and Annie were enjoying dinner at the home of Reverend James Corby and his wife Viola. Two ladies from the church had volunteered to meet the dinner needs of the boys. The Corby's had been married for over thirty years and from all appearances were more in love than ever. Viola was a gracious woman whose looks matched her caring heart. She was very popular with the ladies of the church and often led Bible studies in their home. She was very supportive of James and walked by his side through all the ups and downs of ministry. Together they had a son, James Jr., who lived with his wife in Pennsylvania.

Viola had prepared spaghetti and meat balls, tossed salad, and homemade bread. Conversation was light and lively and sprinkled with humorous stories and quips. Life with the boys was woven through several of the topics with the agreement that the four of them were special men in their own way.

After dinner the two couples were seated in the living room enjoying a slice of chocolate cake. Greg and Viola also had a cup of decaffeinated coffee. Viola sat on the couch with Greg and Annie while James settled into the recliner.

Extending his index finger toward the ceiling Pastor Corby announced, "Now those boys are a part of our community, and we're gonna do what we can to help them."

"I'm afraid the state may have more to say about it than we do," Annie haltingly replied.

Greg leaned forward adding, "All the guys need is a place to stay and someone to look after them. They're fairly self-sufficient."

James and viola nodded in agreement.

"Greg and I are going to stay with them until the state makes a decision," Annie explained. "The house is in bad shape and Social Services doesn't have the money to fix it up so they're gonna have to close it down and move the guys somewhere else. There's a good chance they won't be together."

"That's terrible," Viola said. "Those guys have been together for so long. They'll feel so lost."

"I know," Annie said. "None of them deals very well with change. Losing Esther was bad enough. But losing each other on top of all that...? I wish we had the money to fix it up, but they're saying it's gonna cost about $50,000. And there's still a mortgage of over $45,000."

"Wow! That's a lot of money," James gasped.

"Yeah," Greg teased. "I'm thinking of going to Vegas on a fundraising mission." Then he smiled and nudged Annie with his shoulder.

"Yeah Vegas! Guaranteed money," Annie said while rolling her eyes.

"I wish we had the money at the church," James added. "But things are pretty tight right now. We just had the fellowship hall renovated and had to replace the entire HVAC system. We'll be payin' on that for a while."

Viola leaned forward and said, "I think the best thing we can do is pray about it. That's what Esther would do!"

James looked at her and nodded. "Yeah, let's commit it to the hands of the Lord. He didn't lift us up to let us down. How 'bout we pray right now?"

The other three nodded and all four leaned forward and joined hands.

Then James led the group in prayer. "Heavenly Father, you know all things and you are all sufficient. You know each of these boys and we know that you love them as much as you love us. But they're in a tight spot right now. They're in danger of losing their home and being placed in different places. That's really hard for these guys. Will you do something special for these men? Please just show up and show off! And we will be sure to thank you and lift up your name in praise. And it's in your name that we pray and commit these boys to your care. Amen."

The group joined together with an "Amen."

Then they leaned back as James added, "Well, the mail's been delivered. Our posture right now is to sit back and see how the Lord's gonna step in. We only see the grains of sand but the Lord is always looking at the whole beach."

The others nodded in agreement. The evening ended as pleasantly as it had begun.

-27-
HEALING STORIES

The next evening, Greg, Annie, and the boys were seated in the living room watching *The Andy Griffith Show*. As was his habit, Robert always whistled, as best he could, the theme song of the show. Just before the conclusion, Annie dug into the couch and pulled out the remote. She waited until the last note was whistled and then with a quick press of a button made their evening entertainment disappear.

"Okay guys," it's time for bed. Greg and I will do the dishes." Then punctuating her statement with an elbow to his side, she asked, "Won't we Greg?" Greg nodded as he shrugged his shoulders.

Robert spoke up, "I miss Ms. Esther. Today's not been a good day. Maybe tomorrow will be better."

Scotty joined in, "Yeah, it's not a good day."

"How 'bout telling us a story Annie?"

The other two chimed in, "Yeah Annie! Tell us a story like Ms. Esther always did."

Greg stood up and clapped his hands together, "Hey, I know a story!"

Turning to Greg Waynie pleaded, "Go ahead Greg. Tell your story. Tell a good one!"

Greg cleared his throat and began with an air of drama. He leaned forward and lowered his voice while holding a serious look on his face. "One day a long, long time ago, there was a sweet, sweet girl. She never complained. She never was mean, and she never gave her husband a hard time." Annie leaned forward and turned her head to the side. She felt a smirk gaining position on her face. Fighting his own smile, Greg continued, "But that was only one day and it was a long, long time ago. The end!" With that he leaned forward at the waist and gave a deep bow coupled with a hearty chuckle.

His laughter was muffled by the pillow Annie was pressing against his face.

The boys all stood up when the pillow covered Greg's face.

J.T. pointed at him and smiled broadly while bouncing up and down on is toes. Robert said, "Oh, Greg. You told that about Annie. She's gonna get you Greg! "

"Get 'em Annie" Waynie urged as he pointed at Greg.

"Annie, you tell us a story. Greg's stories are no good," Scotty begged.

"Alright. Now that the knucklehead among us is finished I'll see what I can come up with."

Waynie laughed and pointed at Greg. "Oh Greg. Annie called you a knucklehead. She said you're a knucklehead. Greg's a knucklehead!"

"Yeah, knucklehead Greg," Scotty parroted.

Nodding his head toward Annie Greg said, "Thanks a lot babe. See what you started?"

"You deserve it," she said smiling while nodding her head. "Now what story do you guys want to hear?"

"Tell us one we never heard," Waynie pleaded, "Ms. Esther always had lots of 'em."

"Yeah! Yeah!" Scotty added. "Tell us one we never heard before."

The boys each settled back in their places around the living room. Annie had their complete attention.

Annie sat back down on the couch next to Greg. "Well, I don't know if I can tell a story like Ms. Esther, but here goes."

"Once upon a time there was a beautiful maiden who lived in a small village with her mom and dad."

"What's a maiden?" Robert asked.

"A young woman," she replied.

"Oh, a young woman," Robert said nodded in understanding, then to the others. "She was a young woman."

Annie continued, "She wasn't just beautiful, she was kind and loving and everyone in the town loved her."

"I can see where this is going," Greg interjected.

Annie patted his leg turning to him, "Shush! Behave!"

"What was her name?" Scotty asked.

"Her name was..." Annie looked over at the desk against the wall and spotted several things on top. "Penita. Her name was Penita and she was the prettiest girl in the entire village. Well also in that village was a young man who just like everyone else, loved Penita."

Robert raised his hand, "What was his name?"

Annie looked over at the desk again, "His name was "Chairo."

"Sounds Spanish," Greg offered.

"That's because it is. Their little village was in Spain. And it was a beautiful country with streams and lakes and rolling hills. Every day was sunny but not hot and it only rained at night when the people were asleep. There were sheep and goats on the hillside and the birds sang beautiful songs all the time. Most of the people worked at the chocolate factory which made candy bars for the entire world. The people were really friendly and nice, helping each other out all the time. It was a wonderful place to live."

Waynie leaned even closer, "I want to go there someday."

"Me too!" agreed Robert and Scotty while J.T. smiled and nodded his head.

"Me three," Greg said patting his chest several times.

Annie looked at Greg and tilted her head giving him another *Behave!* look he had grown accustomed to.

 "Well, Chairo was a fairly handsome man and he worked very hard in the fields every day."

Before they could ask, Annie glanced over at the source of names and said, "His boss's name was...El Desko. He was a nice man and he and Chairo were friends spending a lot of time working together. They grew corn, lettuce, and tomatoes."

"I like corn!" Waynie declared.

"Me too!" said Scotty. "It's my favorite."

Before Greg could jump in, Annie gave him *the look.* He just grinned back at her.

"Well, even though Chairo worked hard in the fields every day, he was very poor so he could never ask Penita for a date. But while he was working, he always kept an eye on the road just in case Penita happened to walk by.

"He loved her, didn't he?" Waynie asked.

"He sure did," Annie replied. "Everyone did. But Charo had a problem."

"What kind of problem?" Scotty asked.

"Whenever a day went by and he didn't get a glimpse of Penita, he would grow very, very sad and tired. He would even go to bed with a small tear in his eye."

"I feel sorry for him," Waynie remarked.

"Me too!" Robert sighed. "Keep telling the story Annie."

"Then one day, As Penita was walking by El Desko's field, she happened to look up and notice Chairo. Their eyes met and they smiled at each other. Then a strong wind began to blow behind Penita and it began to push her toward Chairo. Well another wind started blowing behind Chairo pushing him toward Penita. Finally, the two of them were right in front of each other. Without a word Chairo reached out and took both of Penita's hands. Then she leaned forward and kissed him right on the lips."

J.T. grinned and rocked back and forth while the other boys cheered, "Ohhhhh! They kissed!"

"But this wasn't just any kiss. This was a kiss from Penita," she reminded them.

Waynie interjected, "Yeah, I'll bet it was a magic kiss."

"It sure was," she confirmed. "The kiss was so special that it gave Chairo incredible strength. And with that strength he was able to work for four days straight without taking a break. Then with all the extra money he had he was able to take Penita on a date to the finest restaurant in the village. There they fell deeper in love and got married and lived happily ever after. The end." Annie stood, put one arm behind her back and one arm in front of her waist.

Then she turned in three directions while giving several exaggerated bows.

Waynie leaned forward. "That's a good story Annie. You tell good stories! Better than Greg."

"Yeah!" Robert agreed, "He's a knucklehead!"

"Thanks a lot Babe!" Greg teased smiling.

Scotty whispered, "I like stories like that."

J.T. gave three big oversized nods, smiled and pumped his fist.

"Yeah, me too! I like stories like that," Robert added patting his chest.

"You're a good storyteller Annie," Waynie declared. "You need to tell more stories like that."

"Yeah," Scotty agreed.

Greg pointed his finger in the air, tilted his head to the side exclaiming, "Especially ones with the handsome Chairo in 'em."

Annie gave him a smirk. "Yeah sure. Handsome Chairo the laborer. Okay guys time for bed. You fellas get ready, and we'll come in and say goodnight in a little while.

The young men began filing down the hall. While bringing up the rear, Waynie looked over his shoulder saying, "You probably need some time to smooch on the couch." Then he made some kissing sounds. The other boys joined him in bursts of laughter.

Greg grabbed Annie's hand and sat down pulling her beside him on the couch. "Not bad Ms. Annie. Not bad at all."

"That's the best I can do. Wanna Smooch?"

"With you?"

"Give me a kiss you idiot!"

Greg embraced his wife and planted a long and passionate kiss on her lips.

"I love you Chairo!"

"I love you too Penita!"

-28-
ELEVATED SPIRITS

That Saturday Annie, Greg, and the boys found themselves in Annie's office picking up some files Annie needed to work on that weekend.

As they headed down the hall toward the elevator, Waynie slid his hand along the desk of the receptionist. It was made of hickory wood with a granite top. "This is a nice desk," he said with authority. "Wood with a rock top. Good desk. Cost a lot."

Greg gave Annie a questionable look. Annie returned the look and shrugged her shoulders. "Yup Waynie, you sure do know your desks."

"That's a good desk," he said again as they stood in front of the elevator doors. "A real good desk."

When they had entered the elevator Greg pushed the button for the ground floor.

"Thanks for coming with me boys!" Annie said as she patted the folder nestled in her arm. "Now let's hit the park."

"Yeah, the park. The groovy park," Waynie offered.

Robert spoke in his John Wayne voice, "Yeah, the park pilgrim. Good times at the park."

The elevator began its descent. But just as it reached the lobby floor, it stopped.

Annie pushed the ground floor button in frustration. "Oh no! The stupid doors are stuck again. Every other day it gets stuck. Last week three people were stuck in here for over an hour."

Greg looked at her. "Well, I'm sure someone will come get us out." Then he lifted the phone from the wall.

"Greg, it's Saturday," Annie reminded him sighing. "There may not be anybody on call."

"Well let's call anyway."

To their surprise a woman answered the call.

Greg explained, "Yes, ma'am. We're stuck in the elevator in the Jennings building. We're on the ground floor but the doors won't open. Can you send someone to help us out?"

"Yes sir," the woman answered. "We have a team just around the corner and I'll give them a call and get you taken care of right away."

"Thanks," Greg said as he hung up the phone. He turned to Annie and the boys. "They're sending someone over right away. It won't be too long guys."

Annie slumped to the floor and rested her back against the elevator door. The other five followed her lead and settled in against the walls. Gently bumping the back of her head against the door she apologized, "Sorry guys. I didn't think this would happen today. Hopefully they'll get here soon, and we can hit the park."

Waynie, sitting next to her, leaned his shoulder against hers. "That's okay Annie. Someone is coming to get us out. They always come. They'll get us out. It won't be long."

"Yeah," Robert agreed. "They'll come soon."

J.T. didn't smile but he nodded his head in affirmation.

Annie rested the back of her head against the door again. "I know. I'm just so frustrated. I hate when this happens."

"Next time we'll just take the stairs," Greg suggested with a slight smile.

"Yeah right," Annie countered. "You do remember my office is on the fourth floor, don't you?"

Greg simply nodded.

The elevator went silent for a few moments.

Then J.T. started tapping his hand against the floor. It was just a simple 4/4 rhythm, and as he continued, he started to hit the floor with more force making the beat a bit louder.

Just then Robert stood up and began to slowly and quietly sing a song by the Drifters, "When this old world gets me down and people...." The words faded from his voice as continued to hum the tune.

Waynie stayed seated but picked up the next part, "I climb the stairs and my cares just drift into space..."

Annie gave a sigh and looked at them, "Oh, fellas, not now."

Greg nudged her, "I know you like this song."

She looked at him, "They don't even know the right words."

Robert said, "Come on Annie! It will make you feel better."

Waynie got to his feet and looked down at her, "Music is good for the heart. Gotta have music to have a good heart."

"I know. I just don't feel like singing right now. That's all."

Then Scotty and J.T. stood up and the three men began singing louder and louder, "On the roof it's..." Again the words slipped from the young men's minds.

J.T. was now keeping the beat by clapping his hands and bobbing his head. He stepped into the middle of the room and spun on his toes.

Then Greg jumped to his feet and joined the others, "Peaceful as can be. And there the world below can't bother me..."

Waynie pointed his finger and filled in the bridge line, "Let me tell you..."

Greg reached down and grabbed Annie's hand pulling her to her feet. When she stood up, he put his arm around her shoulder. She surrendered with a slight smile and began to sway with him.

Being led by Greg, all the men were now smiling and singing loudly, "When I come home feeling tired and beat..."

Then Annie gave a grin and joined the group, "I go up where the air is fresh and sweet. I get away from the bustlin' crowd and all that rat race noise down in the street."

Then Greg and Annie leaned forward. Greg said, "We got this part guys. On the roof's the only place I know, where you just have to wish to make it sooooo.....Let's go up on the roof."

The young men joined them in singing, "On the roof."

Then Annie stepped into the circle and said loudly, "I got it guys! At night the stars put on a show for free..."

Without her knowing it, the doors behind her opened.

Then Annie belted out, "And darlin' you can share it all with me." Annie kept on singing as she turned to face the newly opened door,

"I keep a tellin' you…"

She broke the song off and found herself standing face to face with an older gentleman. He was wearing jeans and a collared shirt and carrying a cane. "Mornin' Annie!"

"Mornin' Mr. Collins. Just came by to pick up a folder. "

"Me too."

Mr. Collins stepped aside, and the group filed passed him and toward the lobby. Annie stopped after a few strides and fell with her back against the wall. She put her folder in front of her face and quietly said to Greg, "Tell me he didn't hear me."

Greg smiled and teased, "He didn't hear you."

Annie shook her head and sighed.

From the elevator they could hear Mr. Collins whistling the same tune. Greg tilted his head to the side, nodded, and smiled, "He heard you and he saw you."

Annie tilted her head back. "I sure am gonna miss this place."

Waynie asked, "That man was your boss wasn't he Annie? I hope you don't get fired."

As they reached the lobby Scolly remarked, "At least you weren't singing top-secret stuff. You can get fired for that."

The group exited the building and headed for their van and the park.

-29-
THE APPEAL

Monday morning brought the entire group to the conference room at the state Social Security office. All four boys along with Greg were dressed in their best suits and Annie was dressed in a mid-length dark blue dress. They were seated on one side of a long table with Mark Dryden sitting next to Greg. They faced four members of the Social Security department who were dressed equally as formal.

Mark stood up and addressed the panel. "Gentlemen, I know I've only had this case for a few months, but as you can see from previous reports and everything that I've witnessed this is one of the most successful group homes we have in the entire state. I think it would be a great mistake to split these boys up. There must be something that can be done."

In front of each of the members of the panel was an open folder which held the reports on the home, as well as the recommendation of the research committee in charge of the case. Henry Warren was the chairman of the committee. He was a middle-aged man with a slender build to match his receding hairline. He had a kind face and a gentle voice. After a pause, he addressed Mark specifically and the others generally.

"Mr. Dryden, I agree with the reports that this is a very successful home, and that these young men have done very well. But there is nothing we can do. This is not an emotional decision. It just comes down to the hard financial and logistical facts. The state is just not in a position to pay for all the repairs on that house along with the remaining mortgage payments."

After pausing briefly, he continued, "On top of all that, we don't have a home with four vacancies. The best we can do is possibly find one with two openings. Please understand that this is not a personal matter. Now the committee has decided that the boys may remain in the house with Mr. and Mrs. Novak until a suitable place opens for each of them. It looks like it will be two or three weeks at the earliest. We're sorry for the inconvenience, but the decision of the investigating committee is final. Our hands are tied."

Waynie tried to keep his voice low but lacked the ability. Turning to Annie seated next to him, he sternly stated, "I don't want to trade my old friends for new ones. I want to stay with you and Greg."

Annie's eyes teared up. She reached her arm around Waynie comforting him, "I'm sorry Waynie. But you heard the man. There's nothing we can do. It's gonna be okay. You'll see."

Mark left the room with the other six. They all were clearly downtrodden. Their hopes were small, but they were all hanging on to a wish for a different outcome.

"I can't tell you how sorry I am," Mark said. "I knew there was no way they would let you stay in the house, and I wish there was a house with four vacancies, but..."

"We understand. And we appreciate your help," Greg said. "We'll do our best to try to help the guys through this."

"Well, I'll still be assigned to look after the fellas," Mark explained.

Annie gave him a faint smile, "We know. And we appreciate that."

Mark shook hands with all of them and headed down the hall.

"Mr. D is a good man," Robert agreed.

"Yeah. He is," Greg said.

The group left the building, got in the van, and headed for home.

-30-
THE RIDE ABOUT

The next three weeks flew by with no unusual activities. Annie and Greg stayed with them. Annie walked with the young men to the bus each day. They all worked their normal jobs and spent plenty of time together at the house, eating, sleeping, talking, and praying. There were even times of song and laughter as they waited for the day that would bring their parting.

They had been given a date for the end of their stay and that day came rapidly. Greg and Annie did their best to comfort and encourage the boys, but the lifting of their spirits was only temporary. The sadness of the situation seemed to creep back in as soon as they had a chance to think about it.

On a Saturday morning, a couple of days before they were scheduled to vacate the house, Greg and Annie loaded the gang in the van and spent the day driving around to the homes where each of them had been re-assigned. At each place they stopped and introduced the young men to the caregiver of the home. Each person was very kind and invited the boys to come in and look around. Greg and Annie spoke with enthusiasm and pointed out all the positive points to each place. Without force, expressions poured out from the guys, about the nearby park, the back yard, a beautiful stream, or how nice the man or woman was who was in charge.

The boys were impressed with everything they saw and everyone they met including some of the boys who lived in each home. The houses for Waynie and Robert were only a mile from each other, but J.T. and Scotty's places were a good bit toward the outside of the county. They responded well to Annie and Greg's words of encouragement, but their disappointment returned shortly after climbing back in the van.

At the end of their trip, Greg steered the car toward Martino's Pizza House. It was the group's favorite. When Annie clued into what he was doing, she reached across her chest and patting his upper arm. "Good call!' she whispered quietly. Greg grinned and gave a definitive nod.

When the car came within sight of the restaurant, Scotty was the first to spot it. "Pizza" he yelled. Then all four strained to get a glimpse of the place.

"Pizza!" Waynie yelled. "I love pizza! Gotta have some groovy pizza! Pizza makes me smile!"

J.T. pumped his fists wildly and bounced in his seat making the guys laugh.

They noisily entered the place causing heads to turn. The place was more than half full, but a long table in the middle was available. As if they were completely alone, the boys talked loudly to each other.

"This is my favorite place in the whole world," Robert announced.

"Me too!" Waynie agreed. "I wish we could come here every day for lunch and every night for dinner."

"If you did that, you guys would be as big as this place," Greg jokingly explained as Annie led them passed the customers to a long table.

Those seated nearby gave approving smiles as the young men found their seats. Several of them caught the eye of Greg or Annie and shared affirming nods.

The waitress came by to take their order. Annie already knew the boys favorites and ordered personal pizzas for each of them along with three pitchers of iced tea. She and Greg split a medium meat lovers pizza and the group settled in as they waited for their dinner.

During a lull in the conversation, Greg placed the palm of his hand on the table, and without warning, rapped out a short but quiet beat. There was a pause and then Waynie acknowledged, "Ohhhh Greg! I got it!" Then he repeated the beat.

Annie gave a disapproving look. Greg noticed but deliberately ignored her. He rapped out another beat and this time all the boys were clued in and repeated it quietly. The beats continued both in complexity and volume. Before long they were repeating beats that were fifteen raps long. Instead of being annoyed, those in the restaurant were impressed and all eyes were now on the long table.

Greg rose to his feet for the final rhythm repeat. The four young men joined him in standing. The beat was very fast and pitted with several pauses. It almost seemed like Greg was trying to fool them or lose them as he rapped out the difficult beat. He finished with a loud pop on the table as if to say, "Follow that!"

Scotty took the cue and began to repeat the rhythm. The other three picked it up and joined him at the exact same spot. They were following it perfectly and those at the other tables were leaning in all directions to get a glimpse of the action. The boys finished the beat the same way Greg did, with a loud pop on the table. The entire restaurant erupted in applause and the boys were grinning ear to ear as they turned in each direction and gave high fives and exaggerated bows.

A few minutes later the entire table was completely quiet as the gang was enjoying their dinner. The joy of the evening was topped off when Greg was told by the waitress that their entire meal had been paid for by one of the other patrons. He told the group and they all broke out in cheers.

-31-
THE DEPARTURE

D-day for the boys arrived two days later. Annie, Greg, and the boys stood on the front lawn and looked back at the house. Greg had borrowed a truck from a friend, and it was filled with the boy's suitcases and keepsakes. The plan was to drive over to each of the new homes and drop each young man off. Arrangements had been made for each of the boys' parents to be waiting for them at each house.

Annie asked Greg, "Did you lock the house?"

"You afraid someone's gonna steal the old couch and lampshades?"

"Right. Bad habit I guess."

Greg turned to the young men, "Well, boys, say good-bye to the old house."

The young men did their best to hold back their tears. Through their sniffles they each quietly mumbled, "Good-bye old house."

Annie grabbed Greg's hand, "This doesn't seem real. I can't believe they're really gonna auction off this place next month. I don't think the state's gonna get much for it. It's beat up pretty bad."

Greg nodded, "Well, say hello to bureaucracy. Let's go fellas."

The four boys slowly turned and walked toward the van while Greg angled his way to the truck.

As the men climbed in, Annie ordered, "Seat belts boys!" while sliding the door closed. The young men obeyed and went to work in finding and fastening their seat belts.

Before Annie climbed in and Greg reached the truck, Mr. Dryden drove up and blocked their exit. He jumped out explaining, "I'm glad you guys haven't left yet. Got some amazing news for you." Another man got out of the passenger side and walked up to Greg.

Mark pointed at the van, "Mr. Arlington, these are the boys that Esther Snyder used to take care of. And this is Greg and Annie Novak. They've been taking care of the guys for the last few weeks." Greg and Annie each shook his hand.

"Well," the man began, "I've been looking for these men since we received the death notice regarding Esther Snyder. I'm from Masada insurance. The only address we had on file was an old one. Ms. Snyder had a life insurance policy with us, and the boys were recently named as beneficiaries."

"Excuse me," Greg said. "Run that one by me again."

Mr. Dryden spoke up. "Well, Greg, Ms. Esther's policy is almost paid up."

"The total amount comes to $44,000" Mr. Arlington explained. "I have the check made out to the social services department as legal guardians." This time Annie was the confused one. "Do you mean that Social Services has $44,000 in the boys' names?"

"That's right," Mr. Dryden said.

Greg shook his head in wonder. "Wow! We've almost got enough for the repairs. Mr. Dryden, if we could raise another $6,000 would the Social Security department go ahead with the repairs?"

"I would have to get that approved by the committee. But it does seem to make more sense than getting rid of a home. We don't have enough homes for challenged adults as it is."

Annie leaned in, "Does that mean that the boys could stay here…. and maybe we would qualify as their home guardians?"

"Well, you would have to pass some tests and go through some training, but it is a possibility."

Greg gave a whistle and Annie exclaimed, "This is unreal."

Greg and Annie were so locked into the conversation that they didn't notice that the van had emptied of its passengers. The young men stood by Annie and Greg with a confused look on their faces.

Annie quietly noted, "We're still $6,000 short."

"We've got a little cash," Greg offered.

"Not that much," Annie countered.

A voice from the other side of the car, "I may have the answer,"

When they turned around, they saw Pastor Corby and his wife Viola working their way between the vehicles. Several people from the church were walking up the driveway as well. It soon became a small crowd on the front lawn.

When the people had gathered around them the pastor announced, "When word got out about the boys' situation, people started coming to the church and dropping off cash."

He paused to let the news settle in. "Some people gave money they had in savings. Other people sold some of their belongings and brought the money to the church. This morning I took the money to the bank, and they wrote me a check. He extended an envelope toward Greg and exclaimed, "When it was all over, the people gave over $7,200. To God be the glory!"

Greg accepted the envelope, opened it, and looked down at the check. Annie busied herself wiping the tears off her cheeks.

"But that's not all," the pastor continued. When people in town got the word, several of them told me that when it's time to do the repairs, they'll jump in and help. Whatever it was gonna cost, it should be a good bet less. You know the folks at church are gonna join in too."

Waynie spoke up, "What does this mean? I don't understand! What is everybody saying?"

Greg turned slightly toward Waynie and the boys. "Well, fellas, it means that there is a chance that you won't have to split up and that you can stay in the house after all."

"Yeah," Annie added, "And there's a chance that Greg and I can stay and be your house parents. Ya see, Ms. Esther's gone, but she's still taking care of you. Isn't that great?"

"Yeah grrrrreat!" Robert shouted, as he posed looking and sounding like Tony the Tiger. He didn't understand completely but he and the boys knew something good was happening.

Waynie blurted out, "This is just like in the movies!"

Scotty spun around twice and ended with a bow. J.T. wavered back and forth pumping both fists in the air.

A NEW DAY

It took very little time for the committee to make their decision. The house was to be repaired, the men stayed together, and with the completion of the states' training program, Annie and Greg remained as the house parents and caregivers for the ones they had come to love.

After a short discussion with Mr. Collins and the other supervisors at the law office, Annie was given permission to remain with the firm on a part-time basis. She would still join the boys on the bus ride to work and would be home when their day was complete. Greg kept his position at the high school. They moved permanently out of their apartment and into the house.

A week later, the work on the house had begun. Several trades were hired to complete the work and on Saturdays members of the church arrived to clean, and paint. The men teamed up and removed the large dead tree in the back yard. They left a stack of wood by the curb for anyone needing firewood and even planted several trees and flowers in the front and back yards.

Years later, Waynie, Scotty, Robert, and J.T., although older, continued to live together. They maintained their jobs at the shop and were still cared for by Greg and Annie Novak. A large picture of Ms. Esther Snyder was hung in the living room and the boys often made comments about her. To them, she remained *the Queen of the house.*

Any day, if you found yourself in Middleburg Virginia, and walked down Bradford Street your spirits might be refreshed as you paused to hear a song being sung, laughter from the porch swing, or a beat being rapped out on the table.

ABOUT THE AUTHOR
DR. STEVEN A. JIRGAL

Dr. Steve Jirgal is the founder and director of *The Jirgal Leadership Institute* (Jirgalleadersip.com), where he strives to equip people for success in leadership roles. He and his wife Pam have three adult children-Joshua, Caleb, and Sarah.

Dr. Jirgal is a 1980 graduate of Gettysburg College where he became a four-time conference champion, All-American, and inductee to the Middle Atlantic Conference *All Century Team* in the pole vault. He holds an undergraduate degree in health education and physical education. Following graduation, he taught on the high school and college level while coaching football and track in both venues. He holds masters degrees in Health Education, Sports Medicine, and Divinity, as well as a doctorate in Ministry.

He has been the director of Sports Medicine at Wingate University, area director for the Fellowship of Christian Athletes, and has served on the staff of Hickory Grove Baptist Church in Charlotte, NC, as well as leading Lakeview Baptist Church in Monroe, NC and Anderson Grove Baptist Church as the Senior Pastor. He presently serves as the Leadership Pastor at Lee Park Church in Monroe, NC.

OTHER BOOKS BY DR. JIRGAL
(DESCRIPTIONS TO BE FOUND ON THE JIRGAL
LEADERSHIP WEBSITE AT JIRGALLEADERSHIP.COM)

The Path of a Champion
Dying to Live
Life Points
Laws to Live By
Principles of Wholeness
Running a Clean Race
Encounters with the Christ
The Going to Bed Book
Intentional Steps
52 Words
Mining the Mind of King Solomon
From the Pages of Qoheleth
Life in the Pearl
Christmas Stories from the Heart
When Kindness Blooms

www.ingramcontent.com/pod-product-compliance
Lightning Source LLC
Chambersburg PA
CBHW050359030726
47503CB00006B/1937